IF

CLARA

IF

CLARA

MARTHA
BAILLIE

Coach House Books, Toronto

first edition

Published with the generous assistance of the Canada Council for the Arts and the Ontario Arts Council. Coach House Books also acknowledges the support of the Government of Canada through the Canada Book Fund and the Government of Ontario through the Ontario Book Publishing Tax Credit.

LIBRARY AND ARCHIVES CANADA CATALOGUING IN PUBLICATION

Baillie, Martha, 1960-, author
     If Clara / Martha Baillie.

Issued in print and electronic formats.
ISBN 978-1-55245-356-8 (softcover).
     I. Title.

PS8553.A3658I5 2017   C813'.54   C2017-904957-7

If Clara is available as an ebook: ISBN 978 1 77056 538 8 (EPUB) and ISBN 978 1 77056 539 5 (PDF).

Purchase of the print version of this book entitles you to a free digital copy. To claim your ebook of this title, please email sales@chbooks.com with proof of purchase. (Coach House Books reserves the right to terminate the free digital download offer at any time.)

Julia

As he fell, his hat separated from his head and plummeted. It was brown and made of thick felt. Down the two of them raced, man and hat, through the yellowish-white air. Head below, feet above, he was a stocky man dressed in a shirt made of rough cloth. On his feet he wore brown shoes. Painted into existence in Genoa in the year 1872, he joined a series of tumbling humans commissioned by locals and strangers alike, people who'd experienced a violent accident and wished to thank the saint who'd saved them.

Despite her intense distrust of me, my sister, Clara, would buy me art books. As she had a great deal of time on her hands and spent much of it wandering from one used bookstore to the next, she often stumbled upon unusual volumes at much reduced prices. She has an astute eye and is drawn to the overlooked. A small book of naive Genovese votive paintings was her last gift to me before vanishing from my life for a period of several years.

We met in a café on College Street, while mountainous white clouds rose from behind the flat rooftops of the buildings across the street and swelled in the blue sky. My sister came straight toward me. As she pulled back a chair to sit down, she was already extracting from her shoulder bag the slender volume. Three years older than me, reputedly brilliant, she has lovely skin, large grey eyes that are sometimes blue, a high forehead, long face, and a wide mouth. The milky whiteness of her skin has often made me want to cause a disturbance, to flail my arms and shout, or else hide from its unbearable purity and calm. This was especially true when I was fourteen and painfully aware of my own body's unpredictability and willingness to betray me. Her gaze, all those years ago as now, was enquiring but arrived from far away, as if she were observing me through binoculars.

I thanked her for the book, opened it with care, turned a few pages, and grinned.

'You always choose perfectly. You know me too well.'

As I spoke these words, I wondered if I still believed that she knew me well. I took from my pocket a small envelope, which I handed to her with a warning: 'I know you don't want this, but I'm giving it to you so that you can tear it up without reading a word, if you like. Mom begged me to deliver it, so I am.'

She slipped the envelope into the depths of her shoulder bag and asked what I'd been reading lately. I couldn't decide which of several titles to tell her about, so answered: 'A bunch of things.'

'Julia,' she said.

'Yes?'

'I'm just thinking how solid your name sounds.'

The note I delivered caused her to shun us for two years. She has since reconnected with my mother and me, though recently she's once more disallowed all communication. *To shun: persistently avoid, ignore, or reject (something or someone) through antipathy or caution.* I think the term applies.

The book of votive paintings that she offered me on the cusp of her first disappearance I keep in a drawer at work, as a sort of talisman. When opened, it reveals waiters falling from windows, farmers from trees, and children from balconies. Each of them, caught in rough brush strokes of thick paint, hangs mid-air, suspended by the upward tug of a saint's gaze, which is lifted toward heaven.

Daisy

I could not see who lay across from me, nor to my right. The air conditioner exhaled, rippling the violet curtains surrounding my bed. We were four in the room. I'd been wheeled in only hours before. Propped up and listening, I felt I'd entered the interior of a giant radio in which stories were travelling directionless, in overlapping waves of confession and demand.

'Who is there? This must be another place. Where are we? Take me out of here.'

The thin, determined voice continued, unanswered.

'I came with my shoes. I can't leave without them. This is an impossible situation. What a stupid idea to make something you can't get out of.'

I waited, my left leg held straight, wrapped in thick bandages and enclosed in a splint. From another corner of the room came a man's voice.

'The Swiss banks are the problem. For three years now my mother's been fighting with them for access to her safety deposit box. She has a key but they won't let her use it because the box is registered in my father's name and they claim that when he died, the procurement signed by him, allowing her to open the box, became invalid. Such unbelievable sexism, that's Switzerland for you. In any case, her battle over the box is what's keeping her alive. I'm quite sure the day she succeeds, her life will end.'

He was a visitor, one of three gathered around the bed farthest from my own. Every so often a woman's voice interjected with a soft clarity I found soothing: 'Do you mind passing me that glass of water?' or 'The cast chafes at my ankle. I must ask what can be done.'

Perhaps our room was not a radio but a hive. We lay like larvae, safe in our curtained cells, each of us healing as best we could in the violet dusk, well-removed from the outside world, which had smashed us on the ground, breaking our bones without explanation. It was the absence of explanation that united us. So I felt. Though perhaps the others believed in God's will. And just as I pondered the possibility that for the others in my room an unknowable reasoning illuminated or further darkened their plight, a voice spoke from the bed directly to my right.

'Too much, God. You are asking too much of me. Please, you close my door. I am scared. I cannot sleep. The back door, you close it or someone will kill me. Too much, too much you ask of me.'

I reached over and pressed the red call button. A voice asked: 'How can I help you?'

'I need the bedpan please.'

'Okay, someone will be there in a few minutes. Angel to 124-4, Angel.'

Angel pulled the curtain aside.

'Daisy?'

'Yes.'

'Here you go, my dear.'

Supported by my elbows, using my right leg for leverage, I raised my hips and released a warm fountain of urine.

Angel, Salmon, Carson, Margaret, James, Yukio, Sharon, Emily, Truman, Rabindranath, Louise, Feodor – they came with needles, pills, face cloths, glasses of water, bedpans, tubes to insert, valves to adjust. They measured pressure, temperature, ratio of oxygen, and regularity of the bowel, creating an order to contain our broken selves. I savoured their ministrations, drops of morphine slipping into my vein, my body relaxing and my sleep deepening.

Each of them was a famous writer, the touch of their hands as particular as the tone of their prose. On my desk at home, on the screen of my laptop, hung the final page of the first half of my latest novel, in embryonic form. What I read alarmed me, and my pulse accelerated. The sentences on the screen did not belong to my novel. The narrator had become a leg searching for its owner. Having failed to find her or him, the penniless leg looked for work and was hired as a boom on a sailing ship. I could not possibly pass off such nonsense and would have to start all over, racing to meet the publisher's deadline.

I woke to the sound of shouting.

'I came here with my shoes. Will someone get me my shoes, right now, I'm leaving.'

The days replaced each other in a tottering succession, and still my swollen leg could not be operated upon. Such taut skin cut open would not close. The violet curtains at the foot of my bed opened, revealing a woman who'd lost her balance inside a streetcar, breaking her femur, and another who'd tripped on the sidewalk, fracturing several bones in her foot. As for me, I'd been knocked from my bicycle, twisting and shattering my tibia. We were the old, the anticlimactic invalids, everyone over seventy but me, and I'd lived for more than half a century. Perhaps the hospital was hiding us from the young, who'd tumbled from horses, motorcycles, or rooftops, so that we not present too discouraging a vision of old age.

The woman who'd lost her shoes could not say how she'd come to be among us. That evening she was wheeled away to a different ward. The curtains separating our beds were once more drawn tight, when into the violet dusk a new patient was delivered, a mother accompanied by her daughter.

'Shall I tell her that you've fallen?'

'I don't know. What do you think?'

'She doesn't want to hear from us. It's been six months since she demanded that we leave her alone.'

'That long?'

'Yes.'

'I shouldn't have asked you to take her that note.'

'That was the time before. This time it was me who frightened and angered her. I used the term *merciless* about the government. I shouldn't have. It was worse when I gave her your note and she refused to see us for two years.'

'I only wanted her to know that I loved her.'

'You had a right to defend yourself.'

'I wanted her to know that I loved her.'

'I knew it would be pointless.'

'You thought so?'

'Yes. Her illness wouldn't allow her to trust you.'

'And now?'

'I'm not sure. There's a part of her that isn't unwell. Or there used to be. Maybe it was all a performance, an imitation of well-being. I don't know.'

'What would I do without you?'

'Is your shoulder hurting?'

Clara

If you want to have any kind of relationship with me, never mention the following subjects: politics, movies, or eyes. I don't take baths, not ever. I disallow all statements about how much money I could get from the government, if I would agree to their terms. It's not catching, my illness. No need for those latex gloves. You won't offend me. I know how unwell I am. For years I've been trying to convince my sister. She claims to believe that I am unwell but continues to behave toward me as she always has, crashing my boundaries, disregarding my most clearly stated wishes, and congratulating herself on her kindness to me, the self-sacrifices she makes for my sake. There is one question I'd like to ask, a question relating to vehicles. I'd like to ask someone who knows about vehicles. What are these pieces of lead I've been finding on the street and collecting? They vary from two to six inches in length, curve a bit, and a clip attaches. Here, I'll draw you one. See? See how badly I draw? If I had a camera I'd take a photo. Trouble is, I'd take too many photos. I could get a phone and use it just for snapping shots of things, but I don't want a phone. Not anywhere near me. Don't touch the phone and it can't touch you –that's my motto. I had one – a phone. Texting was too easy. Send, send, send. Someone knows more about you than you ever intended. Non-retractable – that's life with a phone. While you're reaching out, other people are reaching in. They fall onto the road. They're always lying near the sidewalk when I find them, but never on the sidewalk. They must drop from cars or trucks and not be missed. Their function? That, I can't figure out. I'd arranged more than two dozen in rows on my kitchen counter, when I remembered Marie Curie. True, it was mercury not lead that poisoned her. Still, these could make me ill, these slightly curved small bars of lead. Cleared from the kitchen counter, enclosed in a glass jar, no longer arranged by size, no longer arranged, piled like bones in a mass grave, lead bones in a glass grave, this is the best I can do as I'm not yet ready to throw them out. They'll keep falling off trucks or cars, but I won't bend down to pick them up. My new motto: no more collecting bits of poisonous matter no matter how alluring. The kitchen is not a place where I cook or eat. I use the electric kettle, I elect the kettle, I trick the kettle. It stands, the elected, much-tricked kettle on the unused stove. Tea bags can be seen drying around my apartment. So much sunlight, said Julia, smiling with happiness. She'd found me a sunny ground floor of a house and I tried to look happy, I did. But didn't she know I'd cover over the windows? Her refusal to accept who I am staggers me. If she weren't so clever, I'd consider her stupid but kind. I've got to get out of this basement space, I told her. I named them: centipedes. I didn't ask for more sunlight. No insects, I told her. They breed in the spring. One more spring in this basement crawling with centipedes, which my landlord claims don't exist, and I won't make it, I told Julia. When I killed them I left them squashed on the wall so my landlord could count the corpses for herself. INFESTATION, I yelled at her, my landlord not Julia. I hate it when I yell. INFESTATION, I wrote on a napkin so I wouldn't yell a second time. We argued over the definition, how many it takes to constitute an INFESTATION. They'd taken the stuffing out of me, as the expression goes. They wanted to get inside my stuffing, the centipedes did. There, I've named them, twice, and I'm still here and breathing, none of them crawling in or out of my mouth. So, I contacted my mother. I had no choice. I couldn't escape from the basement, not on my own. Julia found me a place above ground. You can live above ground now, like the rest of us. Very generous, my family members are. They consider me almost human. No. They are generous. They are. But none of this is my fault, none of it, I did not choose illness, nor is it my fault Julia cannot remember what Alice did to her and that she sides with Alice. We were subjected. Upon us they experimented. I don't remember what tests were performed. What aroused them was our confinement, their control over our bodies. They measured response time, the sounds that burst from us, and the sounds that dribbled. Oh, exclaimed Julia, such great windows, so much light, what a charming apartment. So long as there aren't any insects, I told her. There won't be, she said, as if soothing a child. How do you know? I asked. I asked because I'm that kind of child, the kind that asks and is punished for asking, tortured for seeing what isn't officially there. The tea bags are fully visible. My goal is to make visible. Anything that if concealed could rot or spawn must be exposed. I cannot accept the festering of damp tea bags. Laid out to dry on various surfaces, the tea bags inventory my days. As they dry, the inventory weighs less and less. My immediate past shrivels inside these square, paper cells. Last week no longer leaks brown liquid, staining every surface it touches. Julia gives the impression of being open because she enters a room with all the disruptive abandon of wind pouring through a window, lifting, knocking over without regard for others. But she is abandoning nothing. The hard kernel of her self-interest, polished, remains nestled. Why anyone trusts a fellow human makes no sense to me. Do you know anyone who has never lied? We trust out of necessity, not because anyone is worthy of trust, each of us locked in our own experiences and convinced that our truth is the truth. When I was two, my older cousins raced each other, screaming with delight, into a pond in a forest. I stood and trotted after them on my pudgy legs. Pulled by their pleasure, I hurtled forward. Someone snatched me from the water. Two muscular arms broke my headlong rush into shared joy. My plunge into the glee of others was intercepted and denied. I remember none of this. It is an afternoon narrated. My mother revives this tale, often. All the same, the scent of pine needles permeates my childhood outside of any narration. The smells belong to me. My mother tells the pond story to demonstrate that I have always been the object of her love, which takes the form of fear. A tremor in her voice, as she describes the pond swallowing me, constitutes proof of love on her part and proof of me as sinking object. It was, however, her narration aside, the freest moment of my life, my fat legs carrying me over the wet edge and into the depths, liberated from their grasp. They'd not had long to define me. The afternoon of the pond preceded my sister. My mother describes the cousins, their long legs and my short legs, all the legs running, to show that I was once capable of joining in, but that the price of doing so, for me, would be death. Then my sister arrived. Alice made a pact with herself. Clara will not suffer what Alice endured, the unjust loss of central place imposed by the arrival of a second child. The attention Alice gave to Julia differed in quality from the attention in which she drowned me. I breathe language. If I breathe at all, it is language I breathe. So many words besides *mother* pile up inside me that her love sinks out of sight and colour returns to my cheeks, as they say. The loose change of language, words weighty as gold bullion, all of it and all of us. I contribute nothing to the economy. People do not point with their finger or lock me in a cage or an asylum, because such behaviour has fallen out of fashion. The mentally ill are negative space. I am the space surrounding those more solid. In the public library, a book of works by the British artist Rachel Whiteread presents me as I am. I opened the book and there stood a giant concrete mould of the interior of a house whose exterior had been peeled off. Air had become concrete, the penetrable made impenetrable, every absent window, electric socket, and door recorded as indentation. She'd done the same with bookshelves: every book gone, and a plaster cast of the air between shelf and book offered as documentation of the book's previous presence. The art of Rachel Whiteread consists of this: negative space is given solid form and positive space done away with. Artists are permitted to repeat themselves, especially if what they do is clever. Politicians and young children understand the power of repetition. To be human is to repeat until an accident occurs. All discoveries are accidental. *I love you*, my mother repeated. *I love you*. What followed was not accidental. It was calculated to unnerve me to the point of muteness.

Julia

As curator, I am too directly involved. I select the works, envision how they'll converse, shape the visitor's approach within the gallery, and then there's the artist's ego – handling such a bomb, I stop sleeping at night; not every artist gives me insomnia, but still.

This morning I deliberately arrived before my colleagues. It always happens this way. A day comes when my longing to experience the show as if I'd come upon it by chance propels me out of bed even earlier than usual and I race across town. The installation must take me by surprise. If this does not happen then I know that the work is lacking.

A set of five wooden steps, painted white, leading to nothing but a pair of binoculars mounted on a white wall. Though the binoculars point into the wall, presumably they will reveal more than white paint.

I approach the steps and unease ambushes me. I raise my foot and feel I am climbing to a gallows or guillotine. The small platform at the top of the steps is large enough for one person to stand safely, not more. I turn my back on the empty gallery; doing so increases my feeling of vulnerability. I peer into the binoculars. A sunlit brick wall, close enough for me to touch, and a portion of flat roof, overhung in one corner by leafy branches bending in a breeze, becomes the visible world. The clarity of the world presses against me. A sparrow shoots across the blue sky. The scene shocks me, as it should. How can I be gazing at the real outdoors from inside a windowless 'white cube'? Possibly the mobile leaves, their restless shadows, and the sparrow in flight exist only as video footage? No. I feel in my gut that I am bearing direct witness. I am not viewing a visual record of what once was but is no more.

Of course, I know the answer. The gallery, originally a school library, was lined with tall windows, which we concealed when we acquired the space, needing for our purposes not sunlight but solid, blank surfaces, and artificial lighting under our strict control. Through the hidden windows, the binoculars installed by our current artist now give access to the outside world. I'd witnessed the installing of the binoculars. My surprise at the disconcerting immediacy of the outdoors scene – the trembling leaves, the passing bird – told me his art was successful.

Across the room a second pair of binoculars waited. I descended the stairs, feeling many eyes upon me though I was alone in the room. I was not alone. In an art gallery one is never alone. Art observes you as you pass through the space it inhabits.

The second binoculars thrust a street scene into intimate focus. A young woman, shoulder-length hair, cycling helmet, abundantly freckled arms and legs, sailed in then out of the frame. Two narrow doors, identical except in colour, one blue, one black, both leading into the brick duplex across the street, did not open. I wanted them to open, and continued to stare, willing them to do so. A massive man with rounded shoulders and a polished head ambled into the scene, from right to left, followed by a Great Dane on a pink leash. Clouds drifted and leaves fluttered as they do on all but the most still days. I could have kept watching. I would have. Either the guilt of being a voyeur or the guilt of knowing how much work was waiting on my desk pulled me away from my viewing post.

I'd sat down at my desk and was smiling in the direction of my colleagues, who were drifting in, sipping coffee, then leaning forward to turn on their computers, when my phone rang and I scooped it to my ear.

'Coffee? Lunch?'

'Lunch.'

'Time? Place?'

'How about we meet here, then go somewhere on Queen? Say, one o'clock?'

'Okay.'

'Come a bit before, so you can see the new show.'

'You think so? You know how little I'll understand.'

'Bullshit, Maurice.'

Maurice

I presented myself in front of her desk, stood mutely staring at her.

'You were gone awhile.'

'Yes.'

'You liked the show?'

'I'm not sure I can forgive you.'

'Really? What for? No. Don't tell me. I'm famished, let's go find food.'

Once we were outside the building and walking, Julia fixed her dark eyes on me and demanded I explain her crime.

'What is it I'm guilty of, exactly?'

'He's divine. The man you invited me to spy on.'

'Was he leading a Great Dane on a pink leash? A heavy, bald guy, with bad posture but impressive?'

'No. As a matter of fact, he had grasshopper legs and was wearing two-tone shoes. Twice he tripped and nearly fell coming down his own front steps. If he'd broken his leg, what would you have done?'

'What would I have done?'

'You're the one aiming a pair of binoculars at his door.'

'No I'm not. The artist is.'

'Chosen by you.'

'Yes. Yes, I agreed to the binoculars. I love them.'

'He stepped through the doorway onto his front porch, in his gorgeous two-tone shoes. His hand shot through the air, flipped a lock of auburn hair out of his eyes, and I wanted to kill you. While he turned his head and looked down the street, I stared at his long nose. He scratched behind his ear, into which I longed to stick my tongue.'

'Go on.'

'You've caused all this.'

'I disagree. But go on.'

'He glanced at his watch, sat himself down on the top step of the porch, and opened his briefcase. Soft leather with two metal buckles. Out came a bible, a pair of handcuffs, a yarmulke, a copy of the Quran, and a banana. Seconds later everything went back into his briefcase but the banana, which he peeled. I watched him eat it. I focused the binoculars on his mouth, on the pale fruit and the rhythm of his lips. When he'd done he stood, trotted down the stairs, tripped, caught hold of the railing, made it down two more steps, tripped again, regained his balance, and walked out of existence, stage right.'

'Did he enter through the blue or the black door?'

'The blue door. His blue door.'

'I haven't seen anyone come or go, not through either door. You're lucky. I was dying for one of those doors to open, but I had to stop watching because of the work piled on my desk.'

'You are responsible for all of this, Julia. I'm going to drop by the gallery every day and stare through those binoculars, waiting for him to appear. I won't be able to stop myself. I'm sure of it. As sure as I've felt about anything in a long time.'

'Is that so bad?'

'It will be if he doesn't show himself again. The rabbit showed itself and the hunter fired his gun. See what you've done to me, Julia. Bang, bang. I want to have him all to myself. Bang, bang. You are despicable.'

'Shouldn't you be thanking me?'

'I will be thanking you by coming every day to the gallery and spying on a stranger to see how often he trips coming down his front steps.'

We'd arrived at the restaurant and were shown to a table on the patio. I opened the menu, considered my options, and ordered a mint tea.

'That's all you're having?'

'My stomach. Anything more would nauseate me.'

'Because you're in love with Mr. Fancy Shoes?'

'Yes.'

'You're in love and I can't decide what to do about my sister.'

'You haven't mentioned her in ages.'

'Because she hasn't spoken to me in over six months.'

'Ah.'

'I need your advice. Our mother, Clara's and mine, she's fallen. Amazingly, she hasn't badly broken any bones, just a hairline fracture in her shoulder. They were more worried about her heart and moved her immediately out of Ortho- pedics, where she shouldn't have been, and into Cardiology, where they kept her for a few days, monitoring her heart and trying to determine the cause of her fall, which was likely dizziness. She couldn't remember what had occurred and so couldn't tell them, which didn't prevent every new doctor from asking her all over again. As soon as they got her medications adjusted, they decided to send her home, though the tiny fracture in her shoulder meant that she couldn't dress or undress on her own, nor reposition herself in bed, not without a lot of pain, as I pointed out to them repeatedly. Hospitals encourage repetition. They relented and sent her to a retirement complex to mend. To my complete surprise, she likes it there and has decided against moving back home. In the retirement complex Alice feels safe and less alone. Many of the residents get parked in the hall, slumped in their chairs, silent or yelling. But others come and go, pushing their walkers, intent on reaching their destination. Alice is herded off to bingo and singalong sessions and movies, though she can't hold a tune, dislikes playing games, and detests conformity. She's become a willing participant, a smiling ethnographer, noting the likes and dislikes, the alarming behaviours and tranquil habits of her fellow residents. Yesterday, a talkative woman, who survived the firebombing of Dresden, then escaped Germany by cycling down tiny rural roads, avoiding the main thoroughfares, where, she explained, the likelihood of being raped was considerable, befriended Alice. For Alice she demonstrated the gestures to make and the tone to use to convince a farmer to let you sleep in his barn. She has also taught Alice how to obtain an extra serving of ice cream with every meal. I doubt this will last, Alice's newfound contentment amongst strangers. It would be good if it did. But soon, I'm guessing, she'll want familiar faces. I've placed her on the waiting list for the home where a few of her old neighbours live, not close friends but people she's known for decades. For now, she's tolerating the bland food, narrow hallways, and crowded, unreliable elevators with impressive grace. Someone comes every morning to help her dress, to ensure that she takes her pills and finds her hairbrush, and to change her diaper. I could hire someone to live with her, but that's not what she wants. 'My time in my own house is over. If I can't live by myself, I'd rather live here.' She's clear, much more so than I am. I'm not ready to face what to do with the house. It's where Clara and I grew up, if we did grow up. So, here's my question: do I tell Clara about Alice or not? She's asked to be left alone. She's ordered us to respect her need for solitude. She's warned us of consequences, should we stupidly disobey. I've stayed away. But now, I feel she should know about Alice. I feel. But what does Clara feel?'

Daisy

I returned home, the leg not mine. I could not accept it as a part of me; it remained alien. They'd wrapped the limb in fibreglass from ankle to top of thigh. In place of my familiar foot, fluid-swollen flesh protruded from the narrower end of the cast, and sent the message 'prickle' to my brain. Bone and muscle had been brutalized. Now, they hid. Two windows framed my world, one facing east, the other west. I watched the branches of a tree sway in currents of wind that could not touch me, and I felt contentment. Time passed. The light behind the leaves and behind the clouds intensified. The sky darkened and electric lights came on. Every day, I hopped between my three rooms. So as not to fall over, I pushed a metal walker in front of me. My hip hoisted the leg, and in this way the foot hovered above the floor. The gaps between pieces of furniture acquired immense significance. From here I could reach to there but not to further over there. If a vessel contained liquid but possessed a secure lid, I could carry it in the small backpack I took to wearing. I sat on the sofa and drank tea. The tea tasted as tea does on the summit of a mountain. Friends brought food. Taking the key from under the mat, they stepped out of the summer heat into the cool of the house. While they visited I enjoyed their company, and when they left my solitude pleased me. Much entered through the internet: confounding, labyrinthine forms to be filled so that I might receive a small monthly sum from the government in compensation for being unable to work, and bills to pay, and experimental films to watch. A Belgian director had recently taken her life. I watched her run up flights of stairs, twenty years old and singing to herself, and I watched her sit naked on the floor of an apartment, eating sugar from a paper bag before pulling on a coat and hitchhiking to another apartment in another city to make love to her girlfriend. The internet also brought me messages requiring answers. For example, an invitation to give a reading and a talk at a literary festival, which I would have to decline, and an invitation to have the staples removed from my leg and a new cast put on once the staples were gone, which I would accept. On the evening news, a female journalist in a grassy Hungarian field stuck out her leg, intentionally tripping a male refugee as he ran carrying his child in his arms. I watched the refugee and his son collide with the ground. I closed the lid of my laptop. I opened it again. An Israeli dance troupe, comprised of fifty men and women dressed in tuxedos, moved in intricate, rippling unison, on and off chairs. Together they formed a whole, with the exception of one dancer who repeatedly fell and sprawled on the floor before struggling to regain his chair. Again, I closed my laptop. I read books in fits and starts. The leg made demands. The foot, when not being instructed to pump up and down, swelled. The bones of the foot vanished from sight and its toes refused to bend. Pumping the foot prevented a blood clot from forming in the veins of the calf, and from travelling upward in the direction of my chest, then onward to my brain, or so I was told. Concealed within the fibreglass cocoon, two long incisions were healing, scar tissue forming, bone knitting between metal strips and bolts, muscles shrinking, sinew tightening, liquids pooling in a drama I was spared from observing. I received only clues: a twitch of pain, an itch, the sensation of something trickling from knee to ankle, the latter a nervous illusion. My buttocks ached from too many weeks of sitting. I bathed while perched on a chair, soaking my washcloth in a deep bucket filled with warm water. This was made possible by Ralph Nguyen or Aileen Baird or Rivka Wechsler, on those days when one of them dropped in and offered to fill the bucket at the sink, then to carry it, then to set it on the floor beside my chair. They were loyal friends. Other days, I stood in the kitchen, balancing on my good leg, gripping the sink while washing bits of my body with my free hand. I could have filled out more forms, and the government would have sent someone for an hour a day, not more, one hour. The thought of further forms exhausted me. I was enjoying my privacy. Nonetheless, for the sake of my friends, who were doing more than they could manage in the long run, I would soon apply for the hour a day of free assistance rightfully mine. One month slipped by, then another. Soon, I told myself, I would search for the forms.

I slept in the dining room. Rivka and Ralph had disassembled and removed the table. My bed occupied the liberated space. A commode, rented by Rivka, stood against the wall. Once a day, she, Aileen, or Ralph, more generous than any friend should be, came to empty my urine and feces from the commode's plastic pail. Were it not for Rivka Wechsler, Aileen Baird, and Ralph Nguyen, I could not have lived at home, not with only one quick visit a day from a hurried home-care worker. I'd have been sent to wither in an institution for the aged. The boom leg, the pirate limb, unready for the active regime of a proper rehabilitation centre, I'd have landed in a home for the elderly, though I am not yet old, only broken. My friends saved me from purgatory.

Books formed towers beside me on the sofa where I spent my every waking hour. Intricate shadows appeared on the walls at certain hours. My mind was free to wander. Its meandering journeys could have enriched or leavened the novel that I'd begun writing before the accident, but instead the plot collapsed inward and my prose became rubbery. The texture ruined, there seemed no point adding more sentences. 'Before' belonged to someone else, to a person I recognized as myself, a person in focus yet untouchable, often seen running or climbing stairs. None of the words I typed on the screen of my laptop held weight or meaning. To continue writing felt futile. I stopped writing. I would have liked to go out through my front door, to descend the many steps from my porch to the path leading to the sidewalk, and hop along the sidewalk, in the shade of the trees, through the pleasurable heat of late summer, until my home disappeared behind me, for good, forever. I looked down at my cast. To escape was impossible. For quite a long time I'd not wanted to leave. I'd lain on my bed beneath the benevolent ceiling, had stared sideways through the benevolent window and looked down at the benevolent floor. The caress of home had filled me with wonder. Now I longed for torn clouds, and movement. I forced myself to search through mounds of words. I was looking for ideas but found none. Though present, they refused to reveal themselves. I did not know where to begin. Who could I trust to select an appropriate starting place?

One early September evening, Ralph Nguyen dropped by with a carton of milk. He didn't want me to have to drink my morning tea milkless. 'I'll put it in the fridge. I can't stay. I was meant to be somewhere else an hour ago,' he apologized. On his way to the kitchen, he handed me a parcel. Over his shoulder, he informed me, 'Someone left it for you on your front porch.' He advised me, 'When you get up, be careful. I don't want you to fall. Wear that little purse Rivka brought, so your cellphone is always with you. When you go hopping around to get dinner or whatever, be sure to wear Rivka's purse. Promise?' Having secured my promise, he went on his way, leaving me in the embrace of his inexplicable kindness.

My name was on the parcel, inscribed in black marker, in a handwriting I did not recognize. I hauled myself up from the sofa, took hold of my metal walker, and headed for the kitchen, where a pair of scissors hung from a hook.

Seated once more on the sofa, I cut through the tape and brown paper. Out came a thick manuscript. The sight of it angered me. Right when my own work lay stagnant, someone, I guessed, was offering me their masterpiece, and either asking me to edit it or to recognize its perfection and write a blurb, a glowing endorsement that would connect their novel with my name and achievements. A letter lay on top.

September 8

Dear Daisy Harding,

I admire your work. I apologize for imposing. You did not ask for this manuscript but I am hoping you will read a few pages. Should this novel meet with your approval, I would be grateful if you would consider sending it to a publisher in whom you trust. The work should be attributed to F. H. Homsi. I am not F. H. Homsi but you could be F. H. Homsi, if you like. Every novel requires an author. As F. H. Homsi, you could become this work's protector and bask in any praise the book may receive, without interfering in the career of Daisy Harding. I'll refrain from saying more. Every novel must speak for itself. If this one requires editing, you will proceed, I'm sure, with the same balance of rigour and intuition that you would exercise were this work your own. I'm sure that I am placing F. H. Homsi's novel in trustworthy hands. I trust few people. You I trust, because of your writing.

Respectfully,
Clara Hodgkins

I read the letter a second time, turned it over, examining it for stains or other clues to the environment that had inspired it. I folded and unfolded the letter, and read it again. The title page of the manuscript announced *Don't Get Me Wrong/La Tafhamni Ghalat*. I opened my laptop. In the blink of an eye, Google informed me that 'La Tafhamni Ghalat' is Arabic for 'Don't get me wrong.'

Forty pages into the manuscript, I stopped to catch my breath. The voice telling the story was dark and disturbing. Not a word was out of place. At times the prose succumbed to incoherence with a disquieting urgency. These passages of impenetrability felt essential. An arresting image realigned my perceptions in every paragraph. That such acrobatic weaving of oblique imagery and narrative tension could be sustained from beginning to end seemed unlikely. I continued to read. Several hours later (how many?) I set the manuscript aside and hopped, pushing my metal walker, to the kitchen for a glass of water. A joke was being played at my expense.

In how many languages, in how many countries, had this prize-winning experimental novel already been sold? Clara Hodgkins, if she existed, could not have written such a brilliant book. Was I jealous? Yes. Were there flaws? Yes, but few. They could be corrected. Did a real F. H. Homsi exist? The manuscript told the tale of a young woman, a Syrian refugee, and her descent into madness upon arriving in Toronto. As Kamar's mind unravels, those who have planned to help her become overwhelmed and step away. She is left to fend for herself, increasingly unable to do so. Two Syrian folk tales surface in her memory and impose upon her. They both nourish and further unhinge her.

Seated on my sofa, poking about the internet, I stumbled onto the Facebook page of Fahid H. Homsi of Montreal, took note of his existence, then changed paths and located two elderly women, both named Clara Hodgkins, both living in the United States, one in Wisconsin, the other in Texas, neither of them likely to have left a parcel on my front porch. Had a digital version of Clara Hodgkins's manuscript, and her letter, arrived in my email box, I would have deleted her offerings without opening them, exhausted by the daily deluge and fearing a virus. But this was different, two hundred pages of print, wrapped in brown paper, hand-delivered, my name on the outside in a round, youthful script at odds with the darkness of the parcel's content. Paragraph after paragraph of unnerving, gouging, carefully crafted prose. I sent Fahid H. Homsi a message by way of Facebook, asking if he were the author of a novel titled *Don't Get Me Wrong*. Within a matter of minutes his answer arrived. He wished he were, but no, he'd never written a novel.

I returned to the manuscript, reread key passages. It seduced me again. It made me weep. In an early scene,

Kamar recalls a leg landing on the sidewalk in front of her. It is her cousin's leg. The rest of him has been tossed onto the hood of a car. But the passages that fascinated and devastated me the most came later. It was the crumbling of language, the chaos of Kamar's mind, allowed to spill onto the page, that moved me to tears. Glimmers of meaning flitted, just out of reach. I read slowly, extending my experience of her undoing. The prose wrapped itself around me. I licked myself clean of a delicious sorrow. I'd arrived at the end, and lay on my sofa, stripped of present, past, and future. I slept. When I woke it was night, and moments from the book were falling like leaves, covering me.

In the morning, I rang up Ralph Nguyen and asked him how I should respond to the person who'd left the parcel. I read him Clara Hodgkins's request, and told him that her manuscript was brilliant.

'It's good, eh?'

'Astounding. Or I think so.'

'Maybe that's why Clara Hodgkins chose you to give it to.'

'Either Clara's not Clara but a friend of mine, or she's Clara and I don't know her.'

'Do you have a hunch?'

'Let's say the source of this gift is a friend.'

'Okay.'

'A friend, testing to see if I am willing to try and pass off someone else's work as my own?'

'They've given you a work already published, but little known? They are joking, or they really want to make a fool out of you. Are your friends nasty?'

'Nobody I know is cruel. I don't think I'm hated. Besides, I typed up several pages and submitted them to the plagiarism site, Turnitin.com. Nothing. It's unlike anything else.'

'Clara Hodgkins may be a stranger presenting you with a chance to become famous. Famous, so long as you stay in disguise.'

'But why me and not her? She could pretend to be F. H. Homsi.'

'Exactly.'

'I think she knows how good the manuscript is.'

'Maybe she found it on a park bench and doesn't dare send it out, in case the real author catches on. She wants to use you.'

'No. I don't feel used.'

'Okay, let's say that this Clara Whoever is morbidly afraid of publishers and publicity but wants her work to live the life it deserves. She trusts you because she admires your books. With each that she's read her trust in you has grown.'

'If she wrote it…'

'Then?'

'I could be F. H. Homsi for her.'

'If she found the manuscript, then its real author, who lost it, has another copy on a USB key and has already submitted the work to an excited editor who has made an offer. The real author is signing a book contract as we speak.'

'I need to meet with Clara Hodgkins. Agreed?'

'That, or do nothing.'

Maurice

I badly want to leave the earth, but for me it's not about speed. I can do with minimal speed, just enough to keep me up there. Skydivers! I am not one of them.

'In a belly-to-earth position, meaning face down, a skydiver reaches terminal velocity at about 195 km/h. Fold in his or her limbs and the diver's terminal velocity will accelerate to 320 km/h, approaching that of a peregrine falcon descending upon its prey. Fire a bullet (size 30-06) straight up into the air, and as it returns to earth it too will attain a terminal velocity of 320 km/h, according to a 1920 U.S. Army Ordinance Study.' Wikipedia.

When I was fifteen I built a hang-glider. Julia remembers that contraption. I threw myself off the top of steep hills and cliffs every chance I got. Dangling in my harness, I'd shift the angle of my wings in response to the air's quietest whisperings, and I belonged. At last I belonged. Then I broke my arm. My mother passed a law against leaping into voids. In my dreams I continued to fly. It took all my concentration, every ounce of my will, as I aimed for the open kitchen window, then soared into the immensity, voyaging above the city, kept aloft by desire, fuelled by intense loneliness. My goal was to escape the weight of my family's wealth, our name, and my father's countless admirers.

Ten years ago I built an ultralight. Two wings, two suspended seats, three wheels, a frame of extreme lightness and strength, also a small engine, fed through a tube from a plastic tank full of gasoline. This potentially explosive tank is located above my head and that of anyone foolish enough to fly with me. 'You'll probably want to wear this,' I told Julia, handing her a helmet, the one time she went up with me. 'Not because it will do you any good if we crash, but because the engine makes a lot of noise. You'll be less bothered by the loudness.' We rolled out into the field, both of us staring straight ahead. The field had been given a clean shave, its grass reduced to stubble. Every bump in the dirt jolted our frame. We rose into the air.

I know when I've separated from the ground because suddenly I am travelling through smoothness. We, the ultralight and I, advance so slowly I have no sensation of being propelled from A to B. It is an experience without glory. That's partly what I love, the absence of glory. I look down. A few minutes ago, A was a line of trees at the edge of a field and B the opposite side of the same field. Now, B is behind us, and we – the wings, the engine, and I – are headed for C, therefore we are moving.

It is rare that I take a passenger along. Julia came that once, but the slowness disappointed her. Today I cannot fly, as there is too much wind. I've arranged to meet Julia for coffee.

Daisy

During the day I tolerate the leg. At night, I fly Air Transat. I travel, unable to sleep, my bed as uncomfortable as a seat on a discount aircraft. Hour upon hour, I toss and turn without destination. Morning brings the relief of hobbling to the kitchen and igniting the blue flame beneath the kettle, of hopping to the sofa and sitting there, fully upright, drinking a cup of tea, while people appear out on the sidewalk. They are newly emerged from the darkness, as I am; they walk along the street, and many of them climb into their cars and drive away, but others continue on foot, and when they have all moved out of sight, the houses and the old school converted into an arts centre remain. The rows of front porches, the windows and doors, and the steps leading up to these, all have been altered or replaced by different owners over the years, the result discordant, as if a record were being played at the wrong speed.

I sit amidst my books and turn on my laptop. Messages have poured in. An old interview, shot in black and white, offers Luis Buñuel, who explains that if you fall asleep in bed while smoking, the cigarette may extinguish itself or set fire to the bed. The cigarette could do either, and Doubt is the cigarette. Doubt sets everything on fire or it does nothing, states Buñuel, unclasping his large hands.

Today, mid-morning, I taped to the outside of my front door an envelope upon which I'd written in big letters the name *Clara Hodgkins*. There is no guarantee that she'll return to my front porch, but I suspect that she wants a response. She's left no ordinary means of contacting her, no email address, or street number, or phone number.

My response reads:

September 12

Dear Clara Hodgkins,

Thank you for your kind words regarding my books. I have read *Don't Get Me Wrong*, and love it. Are you the author of this manuscript? If you are, I would like to meet with you to discuss the work and to talk about what role I might play in placing the manuscript in the hands of an appropriate publisher. I feel strongly that this work deserves to be published, and I thank you for giving me the opportunity to read it, whatever the outcome of our exchange. I should make clear that if you are not the author, if this is a found manuscript or one given to you by someone else, then I cannot see how I could proceed without written permission to do so from the author of the work. I assume that the pseudonym F. H. Homsi is your invention? Should you wish to meet, may I propose Clafouti, a small bakery/café

on Queen Street West, facing Trinity Bellwoods Park?
I could meet you there next Tuesday at 4 p.m.

Regards,
Daisy Harding.

At noon, Ralph dropped by with a jar of cold soup and a salad for two. He let himself in using the key from under the mat.

'The letter taped to your door, you put it there and you want it there, I'm guessing?' he asked, poking his head into the living room.

'Yes. If it says *Clara Hodgkins*, I do.'

'It does.'

'Good. Tell me how you are, dear Ralph.'

'Not good. There's been a minor flood.'

His voice sounded delicate and weary, as if he were made of smoke, as if he were being exhaled by a presence larger than either of us, a presence balancing a cigarette between two immense fingers. Ralph slipped into the kitchen to get forks and spoons, two bowls and two plates.

'Where is the flood?' I called from the sofa.

'At work.' His words floated back to me. 'A pipe burst, two computers got soaked. I've successfully retrieved nearly everything from the hard drives. It took me all night.'

He brought in the tray and set it on the low, oval coffee table.

'But the main server,' he explained. 'If it had gone, there was no backup. Six years' worth of budgets and other records, and no secondary storage system ever put in place. I start trembling just thinking about it.'

He passed me my soup, his hand unsteady.

'Who should have made sure there was backup?'

'Me.'

'Who'd have been responsible if everything had been lost?'

'Me.'

'Ah. I see.'

'Yes.

'And? You did nothing to prevent this because…?'

He leaned forward, eyes alert, a nihilistic amusement occluding his fear.

'When they hired me, nothing was in place. I kept intending to create a backup system, but it repeatedly slipped to the bottom of my list. There was always a deadline, another urgency. You know how it is? You're running up a mountain, and the summit turns out not to be the summit, so you keep running, and now you are too high and the little stones under your feet start slipping, and the sun is setting and you hope you will wake up soon. Creating a backup system, as well as getting all the rest done, I'll be working crazy hours. Let's not talk about me. How's the pirate limb?'

'Hard to say. Presumably healing. It's not causing me much pain and nothing's trickling out, and the foot stops swelling when I pump it back and forth.'

I pumped the foot to demonstrate.

'Looks like you're trying to stop your car on black ice.'

'I am.'

'Aren't we all?'

He set down his empty soup bowl and contemplated me.

'But how are you, Daisy? I mean, how are you really? I expected you to go out of your mind with boredom, but look at you.'

I returned Ralph's inquisitive gaze. I think that's what I did. I rarely know what my face expresses. As for the words that come out of my mouth, they feel even less reliable. For better or worse, this is what I told him:

'I like being confined. I don't want to go out. There's so much to see when you can't move. Light shifts, patterns form and dissolve on indoors walls, outdoors a bending branch suggests the presence of wind, a car drives off, a person who walks by has decided to wear a green sun hat and black shorts today. When, by necessity, you do move to a new room or to a different spot in the same room, a great weight hangs and swings with you. Furthermore, each time you undertake to voyage across a room, the weight and shape of any additional object that you try to carry with you must be given your full consideration as it may alter your equilibrium. Remaining upright is your goal. If you fall, the world will come to an end. The sound of air being released by a vent in the floor or of water flowing from the kitchen tap – these become large happenings, and time slows down.'

'Ah, I see.'

'But there have been days, recently, when the sky looked very alluring, and I felt these three rooms shrinking, and I did want to drag myself out the front door on my bum and down the stairs on my bum, and then what?'

'Exactly,' whispered Ralph in his delicate, exhausted voice. He leaned toward me, as if confiding that our bed was on fire. 'And then what? That's exactly the question. isis, global warming, and then what?'

He leaned closer, and the story he told me was one that I too had heard on the morning news:

The police ordered a man to drop his weapon. He was standing in the stairwell of the subsidized housing complex where he lived. It was a building that provides apartments for people suffering from trauma. He was holding a hammer. A few days earlier he'd graduated from a community college as a certified builder. Soon he would earn a better wage and soon he would send more money back to his wife and children, and soon they would be allowed to join him in this new country of opportunity. Soon. Not too soon but soon. Meantime, he'd gone upstairs to ask his neighbour to turn down her radio, and he took his hammer with him when he went to discuss his unhappiness and frustration. His anger, and his size, and his hammer frightened her, so she slid her telephone from her pocket and called the police. A friend of his, hearing the altercation, came down the hall to speak to him, and he followed his friend's lulling voice out into the hall. The two of them stood talking in the stairwell, while the radio in the woman's apartment continued to vomit its chatter and music, and he hungered to make a loud noise, a noise that would carry, a noise capable of silencing the radio, so he brought his hammer down on the metal railing of the stairwell, and he did so repeatedly. He was listening to the sound that his hammer made, he was feeling the whacking reverberate through his body, when a female police officer followed by a male police officer came running up the stairs. They stopped a few feet below him. They stood in their uniforms and ordered him: 'Drop your weapon.' He held on to his hammer and did nothing because he could not decide what to do or to say, his head full of hammering, chatter, and music, sadness also, and anger, and yes, he did feel fear but of the wrong sort, the sort that makes you hold on to your hammer instead of dropping it. How can you choose what sort of fear to feel? They repeated their command: 'Drop your weapon.' He failed to drop his hammer. The male police officer shot him dead.

Ralph's voice was a soft voice. It travelled with a lightness barely altered by the weight of the story he told. I often wanted to capture and examine and keep for myself the peculiar lightness of his voice. I hoped he would continue speaking so that I could listen longer to his voice, but I knew from the radio that the story he'd just told (which I've now told you) did not have another ending and stopped where it stopped, in a stairwell, though the sound of what had occurred in the stairwell must have carried through the air for quite some time, the acoustics of most stairwells being what they are.

While Ralph told me about the murder of the man with the hammer and I listened, the envelope intended for Clara Hodgkins dangled, undisturbed, taped to my door.

'Do you think she'll take it?' Ralph asked, as he cleared away our soup bowls and salad plates, our cutlery and crumpled paper napkins.

'I do,' I told him.

He said he must leave, and he left, and I closed the door behind him. The door was made of wood except for its upper portion. Through this window I watched him unlock his bicycle from a metal post that was holding a red 'stop' sign in the air. When he had glided down the street and out of sight, I returned to my sofa.

Julia

My mother keeps asking, have I spoken with Clara? No, I tell her. Clara hasn't got a telephone. But soon I'll go knock on her door. If she doesn't answer, I'll leave a note, I promise. I promise Alice that I'll visit Clara, and I want to visit Clara, and I am frightened.

I've been remembering *The Day of the Mouse, the Needles, the Magic Show, and My Mother's Imaginary Heart Attack*. That would be the awkward title of the video I'd make, were I a videographer, and the opening image would be of a mouse dropped into the present by digital means, a very fat mouse snatched from twenty years earlier in my life. *The Day of the Mouse, the Needles, the Magic Show, and My Mother's Imaginary Heart Attack* (a day so peculiar it deserves a title), as it unfolded a year ago, took on a weight of the sort impossible to explain. Elements of opaque significance converged. That day convinced me that my sister was more ill than I'd allowed myself to recognize until then. It also tempted me to believe in her visions.

First element uniting present and past: a round room, in a round building – Convocation Hall, University of Toronto. The mouse was obese. It stared down at us. We were over a thousand students. The mouse beseeched us from the screen at the front of the lecture hall. It did not know when to stop eating; a part of its brain had been removed. To make clear that the mouse was of monstrous size, the scientists had placed the swollen, furry animal on a metal tray, which held the creature aloft while its weight was measured and recorded. In its dark eyes I perceived perplexity. When I could no longer endure its gaze, I shifted mine. To know that the mouse's suffering was wilfully imposed became unbearable. I felt I was about to faint and lowered my head between my knees. After a minute or two in this position, I got up and ran from the lecture hall.

Later, twenty years later, I returned to the same hall, not to attend a survey course in psychology, but to hear a pianist whose playing I adored. At every opportunity, I went to hear her. The pianist's performance was listed as one of many diverse and brief offerings in a daylong program of entertainment that promised to include literary readings, talks on various subjects, musical acts, and even a magic show.

Quite sure that I would not stay for more than a few presentations, I climbed to the balcony and selected a seat at the end of a row, one that I could leave from without causing a disturbance.

Soon enough the pianist appeared onstage. Her performance ended too quickly. I could have listened to her all day. Next, a magician, nervous and wearing a black velvet evening jacket several sizes too small, was introduced. He explained that the act he'd chosen was rarely performed. It dated from the nineteenth century and involved several needles, which he displayed, each of them stuck in a small cushion resting on the palm of his hand. He held his arm outstretched so we might see the needles clearly. In response to his request for a volunteer, a woman in the audience waved her hand. She was asked to join him onstage. The magician shook her hand, then indicated where he wished her to stand. The magician turned to the audience. 'In a moment,' he announced, 'I am going to ask this gracious volunteer to take one of these needles and stick it in my eye. This will not hurt me, I assure you.' I covered my ears, got up from my seat in the balcony, and ran down the narrow stairs that led to the main foyer and to a tall door that released me onto the sidewalk. I was delivered into the cool air of an early October afternoon. As my feet carried me to the nearest café, my breathing quieted but my mind remained agitated. I entered the café, secured a window seat, and ordered a cup of tea. Several minutes passed. The tea tasted soothing. Why I reached into my shoulder bag and turned on my cellphone, I don't know. It was and is a device I keep with me but turned off, as a rule, unless I'm expecting a pre-arranged call. Why I took it out, I can't say. Within seconds it started ringing, its frantic insistence designed to leave me no choice but to answer. I lifted it to my ear. My mother's voice, breathless, pleaded for me to come as quickly as I could. She believed she might be having a heart attack. I asked her to describe her symptoms. Often she suffered from indigestion, which caused pains in her chest. Most real pain Alice endured with stoic calm, whereas imaginary catastrophes caused her to panic. Therefore, the more alarmed she sounded, the less inclined I was to take her seriously. Her description of her present symptoms convinced me that, despite her fear that her heart might stop beating at any moment, in truth it could withstand her emotions and was not in danger of stopping. Clara, she explained, had just walked out on her, threatening never to speak to her again. 'What happened?' I asked, as I got up and left the café, abandoning my tea on the table. Phone pressed to my ear, I walked along the sidewalk, headed for the nearest subway station. I repeated my question: 'What happened? Did you say something to upset her?'

'Clara came and then she left. Yes, I must have said something, I don't know, something that upset her, yes, I suppose I must have, I don't understand.'

'What did you say?'

'I'm not sure what exactly. Perhaps I mentioned Kathleen's operation. Yesterday, my friend Kathleen came to see me, and the whole time all she spoke about was her eyes, and her fear of going blind, should the operation be unsuccessful. I told this to Clara. Clara asked what I'd been doing all day, and what I'd been doing was listening to Kathleen describe her fears, so out they came. Clara stood up, furious. She shouted at me. She'd warned me not to speak about eyes, she yelled, she'd warned me not to do so, not in her presence, not under any circumstances, and that if I did, she'd turn her back on me. As she ran down the front path, Clara called over her shoulder, 'I want nothing more to do with you. Your promises are worthless. You can't be trusted."

Through the telephone, which I held pressed to my ear, I listened to my mother sobbing. 'It will be all right,' I promised her. 'Clara will calm down. She'll speak to you again. Maybe not tomorrow, but she will. I'm on my way to your place. Breathe slowly. You are not having a heart attack. Does your chest hurt?'

'Not now.'

'Good. Sit down, breathe slowly. Clara will visit you once she's less upset, and when she does you must not mention eyes, no matter what. If you feel pain in your chest before I arrive, call 911.'

I descended the stairs into the subway station, descended further to the platform, the train pulled in, and I slipped inside its reassuring confinement and certainty of purpose.

As I was climbing Alice's front steps, she opened the door. She'd been watching for me. She stood in front of me weeping. She did not often cry. I pulled her to me and felt her shake in my arms. We went indoors, sat down, and I asked her the same questions I'd put to her on the telephone, to which she gave her same answers. When I suggested that she do so, she stretched out on her sofa, and I covered her with a blanket, set a glass of water on the side table, and hoped she might sleep for a while.

My next stop was Clara's apartment. From the outside, little appeared to have changed since the last time I'd visited. As before, an expanse of thick fabric hung in the wide window to the left of the door, ensuring that no curious eyes peer in. The moment I knocked, she opened the door.

'I've come from Mom's,' I told her. 'What exactly happened?'

'She asked for it. She decided to torment me the way she's always done. She couldn't resist the pleasure of seeing me fall apart. I told her I was no longer willing to submit to her designs, that I'd given her the opportunity to show me she could behave, but she'd blown it. She'd done her best to destabilize me, ignoring my requests and warnings, treating me exactly as I'd asked her to refrain from doing. To add insult to injury, she had the nerve to pretend to be confused, as if my anger were unprovoked, a random bolt of lightning striking her innocent self. She's quite the comedian.'

'She mentioned eyes, and her friend's operation?'

'Don't you start!'

'I won't. I'm sorry.'

'Come inside, come on in.'

I stepped into Clara's hallway.

'I don't want to upset you. I've not wanted to tell you this, but now that Alice has behaved the way she has, I've got no choice. She's made it so I have no choice. I want you to understand why I can't bear it when she mentions eyes. You remember when I was little, four or five years old, and I was sent for an operation? You'd have been one or two, so you probably don't remember. But you've heard the story, I'm sure.'

'Yes, I think I know the story. I got to wear your apron while you were away, and, according to Alice, I felt important and happy, standing on a stool, helping to wash the dishes, or rather splashing my hands about in a tub of warm water full of soap bubbles, which Alice put next to the sink. I'd stolen your role as helper, and I didn't miss you. Or so the story goes.'

Clara took a breath. 'And why can't Mom help herself from telling it over and over? Well, it's a convenient cover-up. What really happened is this. I wouldn't hold still while Alice was reading to me. Alice took her pincushion and threatened me. She told me she'd stick a pin in my eye if I didn't hold still. I must have continued to wriggle about because she acted on her words, using a sewing needle. To hide what she'd done, she claimed I had a lazy eye and sent me to the hospital, where the surgeons fixed my eye as best they could.'

I stood in my sister's hallway, picturing the scene she'd just inserted into my childhood, a vision of horror in which my mother behaved with unfathomable cruelty. I could think of nothing to say. A few hours earlier I'd fled a pincushion-wielding magician. My sister believed in her tale, in its every detail. So unwavering was her faith in her vision that I wanted to defend it as real, and to do so with a ferocity equal to hers. But to credit her scenario would have required that I see a sociopath hiding inside Alice, our mother, and this I could not do. I remained silent.

'I'm sorry,' said Clara in response to my silence. 'I didn't want to have to tell you. But this time, she's given me no choice. There's a lot more, best forgotten. I try to keep you safe from the rest of what she did, the other tortures she used on me. Things with insects you don't need to know about. I do my best to spare you. I'm sorry. I'm so sorry, Julia.'

'You needn't be sorry,' I told her, but looked away.

'I'll talk to her again,' Clara offered. 'Not yet, but in a few weeks, if she can behave. Please tell her that if she can behave, I'll talk to her, but if she pulls this sort of shit again, I'm done with her.'

'I'd better get going.'

'Thanks for coming over. I'm sorry you're stuck in the middle of this.'

'Yes, well. That's how it is. I'm glad you're okay. I'll let Alice know that you may be willing to speak with her again, and that she must not mention subjects that you've asked her to avoid.'

I went down the steps to the sidewalk and turned left. I could have headed in the opposite direction, as I had no destination in mind. My sister is insane – this idea landed like a large magnet in the centre of my consciousness and drew everything toward it: the aged maple trees, the advancing clouds, the bus shelter, the shorn grass, the narrow houses pressed tight, and the passing cars. Why, I wondered, had I resisted recognizing her madness until this moment? What obstinacy had prevented me from seeing her clearly? No singular answer offered itself. I would have to pick at the multiple strands of my fears and loyalties in order to comprehend my failure to perceive the obvious. But nothing about Clara was obvious.

Daisy

F. H. Homsi's manuscript waits for me on the sofa, and within the manuscript waits 'The Tale of Our Lady Namlush.' Also, 'The Tale of the Girl and the Judge.' Which of these two Syrian stories disturbs me more? I can't decide.

The envelope for Clara Hodgkins was taken three days ago. I must have been in my kitchen, balancing on one foot with the help of my two crutches (I've exchanged the cumbersome security of my four-legged walker for the relative ease and speed of crutches), when Clara came up onto my porch, tore off the tape, and removed the envelope. Now, I am waiting for her answer.

This morning the surgeon and his assistants examined the leg. Aileen Baird drove me. At the hospital, a young man sliced lengthwise through my cast, using an electric tool that resembled a vibrating pizza-cutter. Next, he pried open the carapace using long-handled pliers, and there lay the larva leg, pale and bloated.

The cast is now gone and the limb wrapped in skin only, but because the limb cannot bend, my brain insists that the cast is present. The limb must not support my weight – about this the surgeon is adamant. No fraction of my weight must be permitted to press down through the left tibia.

My thumbs inch along the red line where the surgeon, twelve weeks ago, made his sinuous cut. I press the no-man's-land of numbness flanking the incision. I've been instructed to work the scar free of the tissue beneath. I put on my glasses, lower my head, examine the dark remnants of scab, which mark the prior progress of staples that clutched and held. My head is a space capsule hovering above a lunar surface made of epidermis. More disturbing than the leg's visible cutaneous devastation is the dull sensation where damaged nerves fail to convey the presence of my exploring fingers.

This morning, I went out into the world. It was necessary. Had I refused to venture out, they could not have removed my cast. Carried at great speed in Aileen Baird's car, I slowed my breathing while the leg stretched the length of the back seat. Perhaps we were not travelling fast. Having lived three months in immobile solitude, how am I to judge the speed of a car? Measurements of velocity, meaningful to others and generally agreed upon, now strike me as arbitrary. Soon, I told myself, you'll be home again and safe; the street life that you are witnessing through the windows of this car does not concern you. The injured needn't join in. For now, you are exempt. Breathe slowly: you are allowed to hide, as long as your extraordinary friends are willing to attend to your needs. When you've consumed their willingness, you will have to cope on your own. You'd be wise to start learning. Begin by teaching the leg to bend. Gentle, the surgeon insisted, gentle motion. Let the leg, newly freed from its fibreglass cocoon, hang over the edge of the sofa. Trust in gravity to pull the foot slowly in the direction of the floor. After a few minutes, or when the discomfort becomes intense, stop. Rest the leg. Begin again. Allow it to hang. Trust. Every few weeks it will bend an inch more. The force of gravity will work for you.

While I rest between rounds of exercises, let us listen, dear reader, to 'The Tale of Our Lady Namlush,' as told by F. H. Homsi.

One evening, long, long ago, Namlush was adjusting her spinning wheel when her needle fell into the fire. She burst into tears and cried out, 'Oh, what a dull, interminable night this will be, now that my needle is lost and I cannot spin! Not only must I sit here with nothing to occupy me, but nobody is here to witness my sorrow!' Soon afterwards, her wise and gentle husband, Baghuth al-Baraghut, came home. Sensing his wife's distress, he asked, 'What makes you so sad, my beautiful one?' Namlush explained what had befallen her. 'But that is simple to fix,' her husband said, and he threw himself into the fire to retrieve her needle. The flames consumed him in seconds. Of Baghuth al-Baraghut nothing remained but ashes. Overcome by sadness, and anger, Namlush yanked out a fistful of her hair. Then she sat on her doorstep, her eyes red, and she waited. A crow, swooping low, asked, 'Namlush, why is your hair all tangled?'

She looked up and answered, 'Namlush has not combed her hair because Prince Zikri has burned to death while attempting to retrieve a needle.'

Hearing this, Crow, weighed down with regret, landed on a branch of a tree and said nothing. The tree, surprised by Crow's silence, asked, 'Crow, why have you gone mute?' To which Crow answered, 'I am mute, and Namlush neglecting her hair, because Prince Zikri has died in a fire, searching for a needle.' The tree, shocked and saddened, shed its leaves. River, seeing Tree naked, enquired, 'From what are you suffering, Tree?' Tree responded, 'Crow is silent, Namlush unkempt, and Prince Zikri has been gobbled by flames because of a lost needle.' River, much distressed, became murky. Goat, bending her head to drink, asked, 'River, what is troubling you?' River replied, 'I am made murky by seeing Tree bare, hearing Crow silent, knowing Namlush unkempt, and Prince Zikri dead in the arms of a fire for attempting to recover a needle.'

The goat, infuriated, knocked her horns against a rock until they broke. 'Goat, why have you broken your horns?' asked the goatherd, arriving too late to stop her. Goat replied, 'My horns are broken, River murky, Tree bare, Crow silent, and Namlush unkempt, because Prince Zikri has been burned to a crisp while retrieving a needle.'

The goatherd, in a fit of sadness, tore his clothes to ribbons. His wife, standing next to him and holding a bowl of beans, asked, 'Husband, what ails you?' The goatherd answered her, 'My clothes are torn, Goat's horns broken, River murky, Tree bare, Crow silent, and Namlush unkempt, because Prince Zikri has died in a fire while looking for a needle.' The wife, in shock and sorrow, spilled the bowl of beans down her front. The goatherd's daughter, who was embroidering with a long needle, looked up, saw her mother covered in beans, and asked, 'Mother, what have you done?' The mother replied, 'I am covered in beans, your father's clothes are torn, Goat's horn broken, River murky, Tree bare, Crow silent, and Namlush unkempt, because fire has turned Prince Zikri into ashes while he was retrieving a needle.' The daughter, much distressed, used her long needle to gouge out her eye. The daughter's husband, rising from his seat too late to prevent this terrible act, beseeched his wife, 'Wife, what have you done?' She answered her husband, 'As you can see, I've gouged out my eye, Mother is covered in beans, Father's clothes are torn, Goat's horn is broken, River murky, Tree bare, Crow silent, and Namlush unkempt, because Prince Zikri has been devoured by fire while retrieving a needle.' Her young husband responded, 'Is it true that one small problem has caused so many tragedies? What foolishness to be upset over a problem so easily resolved. Leave this to me.' Her husband then caught a flea and married it to Namlush, wishing them both a joyful and prosperous life together. Namlush, whose name means flea, rejoiced by combing and braiding her hair. She even stuck a flower in one of her braids. Seeing Namlush looking so lovely, Crow cawed loudly, River listened and became pure, Goat tasted river's clear water and grew new horns in celebration, the delighted goatherd removed his tattered clothing and put on his best outfit, his wife, seeing her husband so well turned out, bathed, then slipped into her favourite dress. Only the daughter, who'd lost an eye, could not undo her unhappiness.

If you grieve, do so in moderation. Celebrate within limits. Take always a rational approach. Sloppy, hasty thinking leads to bad results. These, dear reader, are the morals often attached to this tale, F. H. Homsi assures us. I am growing dangerously fond of F. H. Homsi. I could say much about the portrayal of women in this tale, but I won't. I have fallen in love with a novel, Homsi's novel. Possibly I will burn to a crisp and be reduced to ashes through my love of this novel. But that will happen only if I jump into the fire to rescue *Don't Get Me Wrong La Tafhamni Ghalat.*

Maurice

I knocked on his door. His blue, blue door. The moment he answered, I glanced at his feet, which were bare. His breath smelled sweet, his lovely auburn hair was a mess.

'How can I help you?' he asked.

'I've come to confess.'

'Are you sure it isn't money you want?' he asked, grinning.

'I don't want money, no.'

'Most strangers going door-to-door are hoping for money.'

'I have a confession to make.'

'So you said. Do I look like a priest?'

'No.'

'Who are you? I've never been good at games.'

'My name is Maurice. I've come from the art gallery across the street.'

'Have you stolen an artwork? Are you hoping I'll hide a large painting in my basement?'

'You're the artwork.'

'Me?'

'We watched you through binoculars. We. Anyone who came into the gallery. For two months the binoculars were aimed at your front door. Several times, I saw you come out and go down the street. Twice you stepped out but went nowhere and retreated back inside. The show at the Kleinzhaler Gallery is over now, replaced by a new show. I kept meaning to tell you before it ended. But if you'd complained, they might have had to shut down the show early, which would have caused all sorts of awkwardness and disappointment. The curator is a close friend of mine. I didn't want her to face any awkwardness or blame. I was happiest when you wore your two-tone shoes.'

'My shoes? They're from Milan. Exquisitely made. I'm glad they've provided you with some happiness.'

'May I buy you a drink? I feel I owe you.'

'I don't drink. That's one thing I don't do. But I'll tell you where I bought my shoes, and you can get yourself a pair. You have a good eye.'

'I'd be happy to buy you a coffee. Not today, of course. May I give you my number?'

Julia

I've not yet gone to knock on Clara's door. I am often the source of her fury. What she needs me to believe, I cannot believe: Clara, as a child, was taken to a university laboratory where tests were performed upon her, and her parents, who are my parents, belong to a cult – this tale her present medications suppress only two days out of five.

Finding the most effective medication has required time. The discontinuous search has taken decades. My sister is courageous. Of that, I'm certain. The trouble is that we've known each other far too long. And we both have the same parents, and when we were children they set a certain equation in place. Not on purpose, I say. On purpose, says Clara.

The first drugs, when she was in her twenties, worsened her condition. She felt grains of sand shifting beneath her skin. She had difficulty ordering her thoughts, uttering a full sentence. One morning she walked out of the hospital, unnoticed, free as a bird, as the saying goes, and entered the nearest subway station, where she jumped off the platform, hoping to end the itching. As the train hurtled into the station, she flattened between the rails. Several cars passed over her, while the train's brakes wheezed into action. She was pulled out and returned to the hospital ward. A new medication gradually improved her condition, and the day came she was declared ready to function in society.

Clara applied for a job in a bookstore and was hired. Without fail, she took her medications. At that time there were still a great many bookstores in Toronto. She worked, acquired a small circle of friends, and led a quiet, not entirely unhappy life of contained distress. Would this attempt of mine to summarize her life amuse or enrage Clara? I am the last person anyone should trust when it comes to my sister. I feel too much awe and resentment. A look from Clara, a gesture, and our mother's world trembled. There was our father. He had a playful energy and a short temper. I adored him. Clara, he frightened, until she became a teenager and resisted his authority, breaking his unspoken rules and our mother's taboos, which were different from his. Clara and our father argued, and our parents argued about Clara. She increasingly withdrew. But now and again, she would open her bedroom door. She would offer advice and affection, the advice and affection I craved. Today, I am unskilled at knowing when Clara's using her threats of self-destruction to extract compliance from me, and when her cry is genuine.

When she worked at the bookstore, she and I met once a week for coffee. I was pursuing my university studies, focusing increasingly on the history of visual art. I had no ambition to make art myself. That I received reasonably good marks and the approbation of several professors surprised me. It was Clara who should have been enrolled and receiving degrees. Her mind was far quicker than mine. My parents were convinced that her brilliance lay at the root of her troubles. Her extreme sensitivity, combined with her mind's need to make logical sense of everything she experienced, resulted in her finding connections where others perceived none. All this had caused her to fall ill, my parents believed. About this they agreed. They also believed that my ability to socialize, and to choose (to some degree) what I took to heart and what I dismissed, defined me as normal and stable. The equation was simple, unstated, and wormed its way inside me: the child who can't cope can't because of her intelligence, therefore the child who can cope can because less intelligent. I can think of nothing more valued in my family than intelligence. I sometimes imagine Clara, recovered and opening a gallery down the hall from the Kleinzahler, people flocking through her doors, *Canadian Art* and the CBC tripping over each other to praise her superlative curatorial talents.

Where was I? I've married. I've divorced. I've produced no children. Yes, I've had lovers, though none at the moment. For children it is too late. This does not greatly sadden me. I'd be curious to hear Clara summarize my life. I'd far rather think about the new show at the gallery than think about me. With visitors to the gallery, I try to be gracious. I hope that many are finding the new show engaging and provocative. I want it to be loved.

When our father died, our mother, Alice, enjoyed living on her own. Yet she continuously worried about Clara. She invited her to move back home. As Clara's salary from the bookstore barely covered her expenses, she decided to accept Alice's invitation. Within a few months of settling into our childhood home, Clara grew suspicious of Alice. When Clara and I would meet for coffee she'd report that Alice delighted in observing Clara's every gesture. Clara described a certain way Alice had of holding herself poised and listening, face calm but eyes hungry. 'She has the gaze of a hawk,' said Clara. 'Yes,' I agreed. 'I can imagine what you're describing. I've felt that hunger in her gaze.'

Alice, the Alice we knew when we were growing up, was a person who refrained from responding until she'd carefully assessed the territory she was entering (in old age she's changed, become more spontaneous, less guarded), and she frequently tailored her responses to ensure they received the approval she longed for. Over the years she'd squirrelled away the approval of a wide range of people. She was fiercely independent but also wanted very much to be liked. This contradiction tore at her. All her life she'd felt she was an outsider. She'd obstinately lived according to her own desires, but discreetly. She'd cultivated an opaque and elegant exterior. She'd denied the existence of certain traits in herself. She had a beautiful voice and loved to sing but claimed to loathe being heard singing. The gentle and accepting person that she aspired to be was unblemished by jealousy, or any desire to dominate, to wield any control over others. Directness, in Alice's opinion, was a sign of crudeness. If she felt hungry and desired an apple, Alice would not ask for one, or reach out and take one from the bowl on the table, but would inquire if anyone else might like an apple, and if there were no apple-takers present, she'd try to convince someone that they wanted an apple, using arguments of nutrition, of aesthetics, or of morality. Unless someone else took an apple, she could not allow herself to do so, not publicly. Only in secret could she enjoy apples if others refused to join her in apple eating.

I had no trouble agreeing with Clara, that our mother was a complicated woman and that knowing Alice's true thoughts or feelings often felt next to impossible. And yet, when Clara, encouraged by my response, went on to suggest that Alice wished to undermine Clara's mental equilibrium so as to silence Clara, thus ensuring that Alice's past crimes against Clara, crimes that only Alice and Clara knew of, could never be revealed and receive recognition as truth, I would turn away, muttering something about the day disappearing. I'd glance at my watch.

One weekend I took Alice to the countryside for a few days of relaxation. What Clara had not told me was that she'd been taking over-the-counter pills to enable her to sleep at night and that she felt she needed stronger medication but had parted ways with her psychiatrist and her regular doctor, and her health card needed renewing. The prospect of visiting a government office to have her health card renewed terrified her. The inevitability of having to do so hung like the blade of a guillotine. Increasingly jittery, and with the house to herself, Clara swallowed non-prescription pills by the fistful. Hovering just below the kitchen ceiling, she observed herself doing so. A neighbour with a key to the house by chance let herself in, hoping to borrow Alice's vacuum as her own had stopped functioning. She discovered Clara unconscious and curled on the kitchen floor.

Upon Clara's release from the hospital, I found her a basement apartment in a pleasant and central area, replete with cafés, bookstores, cinemas, galleries, and grocery shops.

All she might need was within walking distance. This was important, as taking the subway frightened her. One of many voices might urge her to jump. Through her own determination, Clara tracked down, on foot, a psychiatrist whose name someone had given to Alice. The overbooked psychiatrist reluctantly took on Clara.

For several years Clara accepted her basement apartment. At what point the centipedes grew in number, I'm unsure. By then she'd decided that Alice and I were untrustworthy. Her landlord made sporadic, ineffectual attempts to curb the infestation. Unable to tolerate the invasion of her small living space by many-legged creatures that moved with frightening rapidity and materialized out of nowhere, Clara eventually risked reconnecting with us, her family. We were threatening, but less so than centipedes. Alice increased the monthly payments she deposited in Clara's bank account, and we found her the sunny ground floor of a house, again in a pleasant neighbourhood.

It is on the door of this new home of Clara's, with its wide front porch and wide front window, which she keeps covered at all times, that soon I will knock loudly. I have no choice. Repeatedly, Alice asks if I have news of Clara. I too want news of Clara. However much I fear her, and fear for her, I too want news of Clara. I would like Clara to come to the Kleinzahler Gallery. Her enthusiasm would be unstinting, if the show appealed to her.

Clara

Boltanski woke. Blinding light and the voice of a policeman yanked him to the surface. Christian Boltanski slept in a car at night. It was his parents' idea for them all to pile on top of each other in the family automobile, ready to drive off at a moment's notice. Their apartment they reserved for daytime life. In his parents' postwar estimation, no apartment was safe at night. They curled in the cramped quarters of their car. Notice the moment! I'm not preaching Buddhism. I'd rather chew gum than go down that road. Unenlightened, peering out of the dark, see the moment scurry under the chair, see it disappear between the floorboards. White noise, from the ceiling fan above my bed, eats all the other sounds in the room. Oh, happiness, my happy, cannibal fan. Consume my dread. Dead without it, dead from lack of sleep, that's how I'd be. Light blaring in his face, his body crumpled and sore from sleeping in a car, he, they, the Boltanskis, survivors of the Holocaust, had reasons to hide, legible reasons. He fogged the cold window with his breath, wrote *fear* with his fingertip. Or he chose a different word. When he wrote *sky* it meant fear, when he wrote *glass* it meant fear, as did the word *toes*. The words I write acquire meaning only by repetition. No singular image of hell comes to mind. *I* fails to contain and to command. The multiples run amok. Family. Write, write, write, and they can't catch us. Hatch me, if you cancan. Ha, ha, ha. Boltanski turned himself into a metal box, and another, and another. He stacked himself in rows, flooded his boxed selves in bright beams of cop light. As for me, I am stocking-tied between the legs of a chair. I am an empty bathtub cradling a burning brain. Let nobody in. Do not enter.

Daisy

Clara Hodgkins has agreed to meet with me.

This afternoon I got up from my red sofa and, supported by two metal crutches, hopped toward the kitchen, feeling pleased that I'd chosen a red sofa, years ago, as an antidote to grey weather. I glanced into the hallway. A paper, fallen through the mail slot, lay on the carpet. The hall carpet, rough in texture and dark grey, I selected years ago for its ability to conceal dirt and to withstand the brutality of winter boots and of salt. Swinging and hopping, I advanced into the hallway and picked up the note.

> Dear Daisy Harding,
>
> I am the author of *Don't Get Me Wrong*. All of it is original except the folk tales, which I took from a collection called *Syrian Tales from the Hearth*. I did not lift them verbatim but modified the wording while remaining true to the original. Thank you for your kind words regarding my novel. I can meet you at Clafouti on Queen, tomorrow at 4 p.m., if that works for you? I will only agree to the novel being published if it is attributed to F. H. Homsi, for whom you may invent whatever biography you like. If these are terms you can't respect, we needn't meet.
>
> Regards, Clara Hodgkins.

I'll ask Ralph if he'll give me a ride to Clafouti, then pick me up afterward. I'm not sure that I can agree to her terms. I may not be willing to pose, after all, as an author with a Syrian surname. Kamar, the novel's narrator, is who she claims to be. She is fiction, and fiction can make whatever claims it likes. Kamar is, according to Kamar, a refugee from Syria. The reader can believe her or not. But F. H. Homsi is a fake, and his Syrian surname lends authority. Kamar doesn't need Homsi's help to ring true. She needs only to be true to herself. I'll suggest F. H. Holmes, a more suitable pseudonym for C. Hodgkins. Clara says that I may attribute whatever biography I like to F. H. Might she permit F. H. to change surnames? If we fail to arrive at an agreement, she may approach another writer whom she admires. I will feel jealous of that other writer. I could have suggested we talk here, in my living room. She's familiar with my front porch. We could have sat together on my red sofa, Clara and I, F. H. observing us from across the room, F. H. impeccably dressed as always, cigarette releasing a thread of smoke, legs loosely crossed at the ankles, far more at ease than either of us. But instead of chatting on the sofa, Clara and I will meet in a public space. The leg has made me less willing to open my door to a stranger. I've become a cautious, one-legged reluctant, who hesitates to invite the world in. Before. Before no longer exists.

Clara

My psychiatrist, Dr. Burns, took me on because I insisted, because I kept walking across the city to sit in her waiting room. I was told about her and went looking for her. I was told she was smart, respectful, and kind – rare qualities in a shrink, rare in anyone. I like her. 'She's got you wrapped around her little finger,' hisses Kevin, and sticks his finger in his ear, searching for wax, one of his more disgusting habits. If I listened to him, I'd fire Dr. Burns. But I won't, because I need her. We need each other. We're not a bad pair. Except that she doesn't understand art and thinks she does. 'Tell your beloved Dr. Burns she's a self-important cow,' Kevin urges me, smiling his most innocent smile, while secretly smearing his earwax underneath the chair.

Are kindness and respect particularly rare in a psychiatrist? I'm not prepared to say. Ask your aunt or your brother. I'm sure someone in your family has an opinion based on personal experience of the sort they avoid discussing. They freed me from the hospital. But before they opened the door and let me go, the shrink in charge sat down on my bed. I felt the warmth of his breath on my cheek and smelled the mint of his mouthwash. I froze. I wanted to move but couldn't. He asked what sort of support I had in place for when I was released. I didn't answer. He repeated his question, in the tone of someone with meetings to attend and reports to fill out, someone who's had his patience tried to the limit by clumsy people who attempt to kill themselves but survive, people who are fascinating on paper but difficult in person, and so I nodded, I gave him the answer he wanted, the quickest one, as if I were completing a multiple-choice exam and not about to be raped. Yes, I nodded. Yes, a psychiatrist is waiting for me in the outside world. Good, he said, and looked pleased, and got up off my bed, and I could breathe again. He smoothed his hair, checked his watch to reassure himself that he belonged to a different world than I did, wished me luck, and walked out of my room. They released me and I had no doctor, no source of medication. Julia started making phone calls. She likes making phone calls. The shrink who'd sat on my bed did not return Julia's calls until at last he grew tired of her panic-stricken messages. He informed Julia that he could not discuss me with her, and asked if she had ever heard of the word *confidentiality*. He would be happy to speak to me, and only me. Julia must never call again. 'Your calls will not be returned.' He was an articulate man, a clear thinker. It was me he wanted. I refused. I couldn't. I wouldn't. 'Tell him to come sit on my bed, I'll tie the sheets around his neck,' whispered Kevin, and I put on my headphones and played Arcade Fire so I couldn't hear Kevin. It was Alice who came up with the name, Dr. Burns. The last thing I wanted was her fingering my life, checking for signs. But Alice is smart and I needed a name, so I wrote it down. Dr. Fiona Burns. And here we are, ten years later, Dr. Burns and I still meeting once a week. Of course she's got lots of others and I have only her. But I try to make sure the equation's not that simple.

Julia

She will sharpen her insults and attack whenever threatened. I will continue to threaten. I am neither dense nor cruel. I threaten because of the news I bring. I am Everyday Reality's unwanted emissary, bearing with me Alice's finances, Alice's medical conditions. I am a reminder that Clara depends upon Alice. I threaten because of a chronic confusion on my part as to who my sister has become. I fail to see her illness as continuously present. There are moments when she seems as before, the sister I once knew. For hours at a time she performs with grace and humour an act entitled *Well-being and Happiness*. Except for the trembling of her hands, her performance is flawless. One afternoon, I raised the subject of income tax. Decades have passed since she last filed with Revenue Canada. Every year they send a letter of warning.

'I really think we should get your income tax done,' I told her, as I stuffed into an envelope the documents I'd spent all day gathering for the accountant I'd hired for Alice. 'For them I don't really exist,' replied Clara, stirring her tea. 'No,' I argued, 'you do. And, in my experience, Revenue Canada can be quite merciless.' She fell silent. She'd dropped by Alice's house, cheerful, talking of poetry and art. Her afternoon in the library, spent leafing through books on Christian Boltanski and Louise Bourgeois, had filled her with energy. Her layered outfit consisted of several skirts of contrasting textures, and two or three tops torn judiciously, safety pins arranged as ornamentation, a striking line of them crossing her hip on the bias. As always, she possessed and displayed an offbeat, inimitable elegance, which I admired and envied. In that moment, in our mother's kitchen, Clara sipping her tea and talking with insight and enthusiasm about art, I mistook her for my sister, a person inhabited by a single, rational self, a person adept at forming opinions, yet open to exploring contradictions. How did I allow myself to forget that my sister, the person sipping tea in my mother's kitchen, smiling, while inquiring what books I'd recently read, was being devoured by an illness of the mind, which caused her to believe that all government organizations were fronts, shielding those whose mission it was to capture and torture her? Was it laziness or disregard, jealousy perhaps, that prevented me from recalling the truth of her condition? What stopped me from behaving with appropriate delicacy and caution? Surely I could have guessed how cruel it was to tell someone with a persecution complex that an arm of the government is 'merciless' and unlikely to overlook them?

To know what you are saying, you must know to whom you are saying it. To whom was I speaking? In that moment, standing in our mother's kitchen, listening to Clara describe a work by Boltanski, a work I knew well and found fascinating, consisting of 686 boxes made of white lead, each box hiding and preserving a portion of the photos, letters, articles, drawings, and other documents collected by Boltanski in his studio over a period of twenty-three years, boxes stacked in rows, forming a wall three metres high and illuminated from above by black desk lamps, whose wires dangle as if to suggest haste, flight, or negligence, and the whole titled *The Archives of C.B. 1965–1988*, in that moment of conversation, I forgot my sister's illness. Or did I?

Perhaps what I am saying is untrue, and I was conscious of her illness in that moment of conversation. Possibly I was concentrating upon her illness, and her wellness, and felt, and judged, that if she was well enough to spend the day reading about art, while I laboured, preparing Alice's documents for the accountant, then she was well enough to contemplate other realities besides art, including the presence in all of our lives of Revenue Canada.

What I felt and thought, why I spoke the words I spoke, in that moment in our mother's kitchen, I cannot say with certainty. Too much time has passed. A few minutes is sufficient time to doubt one's own motives, and months can bring clarity or greater confusion when one's unstated goals are the subject of contention. Clara accused me of cruelty, and for the next six months refused all contact. I wished she'd chosen a softer word than *cruelty*, just as she wished that I had chosen a softer word than *merciless*.

Clara

Only by pretending to be Julia was I able to write a novel. It is my novel, not hers. She does not know it exists. Language is not at odds with Julia. For her it does not break apart midway through a sentence. By telling myself, 'You are Julia,' repeatedly, 'You are Julia,' I tied the many strands together, used knots to create a narrative in the shape of a net. See Kamar thrashing, caught in my plot? I am a loaf that tastes of fish. When Julia tells a story, other voices do not subvert her enterprise. I will not write another novel. It was Dr. Burns who urged me to aim for coherence. *Don't Get Me Wrong*, that's all, that's it, already Kevin's whispering in my ear, 'You little shit,' while pinching Annabel, whose only defence is to wail. Fucking proliferation of emotion. Everyone's desire keeps poking in, pretending to be a thought. The dialogue spews. Don't stop writing, stick to the page, ink scratch on paper, dry as can be, pattern begetting pattern until the voices, crushed under the weight of the written, can do no more than whisper. 'Kill yourself,' they whisper. 'Use the knife in the kitchen.' Instead, I remain seated at my typewriter, pounding. They slide their soft insistence. 'Pills you've already tried. Let's see you succeed this time. Surprise us, use a rope.' Each key is marked with a letter. I AM MADE OF WAX. Capitals must not be overused or the paper goes deaf. I'm not writing to be heard by anyone but this sheet of paper. Let Kamar pursue the thankless task of being understood. I'm happier when my sentences shut themselves tight. I dream of lids, not liftoff. The raw, unspeakable world unwinds. For each dream, paper takes the hit.

Daisy

'Clara?'

It was her nervousness that made me guess who she was, also her eyes. Eyes of an oceanic intensity, weather-station eyes – they matched my idea of her. I smiled.

'Daisy?'

'Yes, I am Daisy. And you must be Clara? You already have some coffee?'

'I'm sorry.' Her face filled with apology. 'I went ahead. I was feeling sleepy. Coffee usually keeps me awake for a bit.'

'I'll go get a tea. I'll just be a minute.'

But the young man behind the counter, perhaps because of my crutches, came over and took my order. I leaned my crutches against the wall and lowered myself into the chair, facing the small table at which Clara sat. I manoeuvred the penniless pirate leg attached to my hip. It just fit under the table. Next I pulled Clara's manuscript out of my bag. The sight of her manuscript made her look away. She gazed at the floor, where nothing particular was happening. I followed her eyes. Brilliant light in the shape of two rectangles twitched on the floorboards. The boards had been painted blue long ago.

'I've read it twice,' I told her, and paused. As she said nothing, I continued. 'I think it's brilliant. Why not become F. H. Homsi yourself, or F. H. Holmes, not necessarily a Syrian, and send it off?'

From her look of panic, I thought she might shove back her chair and rush out of the café.

I assured her, 'I read your letter: the author must be F. H. Homsi. I'm not disagreeing, just curious to know why.'

Already she'd been sitting very straight in her chair, now she pulled herself even taller.

'If it weren't for Kamar, you wouldn't be here talking to me. I invented her and you believed in her enough to come here. If Kamar weren't a Syrian refugee, you wouldn't have cared about her. People have decided that Syrian refugees exist. In a while they'll tire of them, and move on to their next cause, and Syrian refugees will cease to exist in the news and on the lips of Canadians between mouthfuls of breakfast. Nobody believes what has happened to me. But they'll believe Kamar. You did. The mentally ill, we're all refugees.' Clara lifted her coffee cup, but set it back down without taking a sip, her hand trembling. She slipped her hands out of sight, under the table, swallowed air, and continued speaking, addressing the surface of the table. 'We're frightening, we don't contribute because we don't have jobs, we're scared, and angry, unpredictable, and landlords don't want us. Kamar and I have certain things in common. But I want her to have an author who speaks her language, who grew up hearing the same folk tales, eating her favourite foods. She'll be less lonely if F. H. Homsi wrote her.' She raised her eyes and stared into mine. Her inner weather had shifted. With a look of confidence bordering on disdain, she informed me, 'If I'd written about me, you wouldn't have cared. But a Syrian refugee? That'll sell, you thought.'

The waiter brought me my tea and I found his presence reassuring. I was no longer a child and no longer accustomed to being told what I felt, what I cared or didn't care about, and what my motives were. Even as a child I'd intensely disliked it when anyone tried to inform me of my own thoughts and feelings.

'If Kamar had not been Syrian, I would have believed in her suffering, and cared. I didn't need her to be a refugee. But she is a refugee, and the country she's fled is Syria, and you might not have been able to write the way you did if she hadn't been from Syria. There are the folk tales, which you've made inseparable from her. It feels right. That's why I'm here. I'm here because this manuscript feels true. I've no idea if it will sell. I want people to have a chance to read what you've written. How many people, I can't say.'

'Excuse me,' she said, snatching her shoulder bag from the floor, yanking the strap up over her shoulder, while pressing the bag to her chest as if its cloth and bulk might shield her, and she headed for the bathroom at the back of the café.

Apart from the waiter I remained alone. It was a tiny room. Outside, clouds heavy with rain carried their dark cargo across the sky above the park, and trees swayed in the wind. On the sidewalk, pedestrians were leaning forward, stepping more quickly, pressing their coats shut and pulling their hats down. The flow of cars proceeded uninterrupted. On the café floor, Clara's rectangles of sunlight were no longer twitching, they were gone. I reached under the table to reposition the stiff limb attached to my hip. The young man behind the counter, dishtowel and glass in hand, looked over and smiled.

'Tell me it wasn't a bicycle accident.'

'It was.'

'Oh, Christ. Not another.'

I told him the circumstances of my fall, the comforting absurdity of it, that I'd been moving very slowly when my bicycle's right handlebar caught on a city garbage bin, that the weight of too many books, pounds and pounds of them in the basket above the rear tire, caused the bicycle to topple violently and my leg to twist as I tried to catch my balance, the bicycle's front bar smashing my tibia. It was 'my' leg back then, a loyal part of me, dependable, hard-working, mine. 'Another few weeks,' I explained to the waiter, 'and the surgeon may allow me to put a first bit of weight on it. Meanwhile, I'm trying to get it to bend, using no extra force, only the pull of gravity.'

Just as the waiter was wishing me luck, Clara reappeared and he turned to the task of putting away glasses, bowls, and plates. The china and glass produced a pattern of pleasing clicking sounds, which I hoped Clara would find as soothing as I did. Clara sat down opposite me, as before.

'I can't know about any changes you make. You can't tell me. Not under any circumstances. Your role, as F. H. Homsi, will be to protect Kamar, to allow only the smallest changes required, and to inform me of none of them. If I knew you were editing my words, I'd want to do something to make you stop. I wouldn't hurt you but possibly me. Even if I can't protect myself, I can defend Kamar through you. I'm not rewriting her, nobody is. She must be respected and heard. But if I keep her at home with me, she won't be heard. If I let her out, changes will be demanded. That's why you're important. As F. H. Homsi, you can agree to a minimum of editing, and not tell me. I've read your books. I trust you to make good decisions.'

'May I think this over?'

In my nervousness, my gaze slid away from her.

'Could we meet again, in two weeks? Same time, same place, exactly two weeks from today, and I'll have an answer for you?' I said, and to calm myself I rested my hand on the penniless leg. Its message was: *You are not in control. You understand little. Allow for the unexpected.*

'It is a novel that should be read. You've written a difficult, beautiful novel. If I do send it out for you, I'll make sure the text is respected. But you'll have to continue trusting me over a period of months, even years, and accept the results of doing so. As I've said, I love it as it is. But any good publisher will want to edit. At a certain point, there won't be any going back. It will go to press, approved of by F. H. Homsi. Homsi could involve you, when there's still time. Homsi could consult with you. But that's the opposite of what you're asking. I have to think this through before agreeing to be Homsi.'

Clara Hodgkins promised to meet with me in two weeks' time, then hurried out of the café. I watched as she walked west along Queen, head held high, straight into the driving wind and rain.

Maurice

'Not bad,' I offered, with a shrug.

'That's it?'

'It's not my thing. Too much going on at once. How many videos? Six in one room? I knew it would feel horrible, being in there with the binoculars gone. Ease my anguish, Julia. Bring back the binoculars. Aim my gaze at two doors: one blue, one black. Only one needs to open. His blue door.'

Julia offered me one of her wry smiles as she slid the upper drawer of her desk shut.

'Maurice, you knew it couldn't last forever. You can buy your own binoculars and watch his door from the sidewalk.'

'We've met,' I said, with as much restraint as I could manage. 'It feels like ages ago, and no time at all,' I added, casual as a stripper.

She'd lowered her gaze and was logging off her computer. Then, pulling her purse out of a deeper drawer, she told me in a soft voice, 'Yes, we've met, Maurice, and it was ages ago. In high school. You're the only person I still want to know from back then.'

'Not you, Julia.' I couldn't help grinning. 'Mr. Fancy Shoes. He and I. We've met.'

Her arms dropped to her sides.

'Oh.'

'Oh! You got that right.'

'You went over?'

'I did. I'm famished.'

I guided her out of the office and into the foyer.

'And?'

'He's divine. The divine Bruce Mammadov. His grand-parents left Azerbaijan for Australia. They bought land stolen from the Aboriginals, thousands of acres of it, and flourished, grazing and breeding unimaginable numbers of sheep and cattle that munched up all the indigenous plants, the plants so adept at keeping the rain from rushing away, from carving great gullies en route. They are as guilty as it gets, the Mammadovs of South Western Australia; they are as criminal as you and I are, ambling over stolen land in the direction of Queen Street.'

The light turned red and we had to wait.

'The Divine Bruce Mammadov knows no red lights! He grew up in a fly-infested hamlet, a cluster of stone houses with tin roofs, erected in the middle of somewhere (if you're Aboriginal) or nowhere (if you're not Aboriginal), and from there he escaped to Milan, where he sold his taste and charm, working as a fashion consultant, and opened a high-end clothing store. But he missed the taste and colour of the soil into which he'd spat as a child, a child running on long legs, kicking stones, and stopping now and again to draw in the dirt with a stick. He would pause in his running just long enough to draw all the fancy clothes he saw on TV, and even fancier outfits that only he and the dust and the flies knew of. In Milan, he'd dreamed of the orange and ochre dust that had coated his skinny child limbs, and he'd missed the gullies with sides so straight they could only have been carved by a knife-wielding giant but instead were made, and extended yearly, by torrents of rain. He missed the months of suffo-cating heat when he never put his foot down without checking for a snake. He missed the airborne arrival of clouds of parrots, who weighed down the branches of slender trees, ravenous white parrots called cockies, who sharpened their bright yellow beaks on the leaves of the eucalyptus, killing the venerable trees, the wretches. Because of missing home so much, Bruce gave up Milan. Toronto can't hold him, Julia. Not if Milan couldn't. What do I do to keep him here? What will become of me when he goes?'

'Isn't that what you want? To be drawn and quartered by love?'

'Yes.'

'What's he doing here? How old is he? Does he know about the gallery and is he pissed off about the binoculars?'

'He's not pissed off. Amused rather. He's a salesman. Are you ready? What do you think he goes around convincing people to spend their money on? He makes them want and need and feel they can't survive without what?'

'A singing toilet seat?'

'Surveillance cameras. Drop cams. Keep an eye on your kids, your nanny, your lover. All that guilt I felt looking through a pair of binoculars, not even filming or recording, and how does the object of my desire, the cause of my spree of voyeurism, spend his days? Remember he took out a bible, a pair of handcuffs, a yarmulke, and the Quran? Remember how he sat down on his porch and emptied all these curiosities out of his briefcase. I think I mentioned it to you?'

'Maurice, I don't remember.'

'For every customer he pulls a surprise from his briefcase, a surprise that will set them at their ease. As if by accident, while fishing for a sales contract, a pen, or his cellphone, he slips out an object that he intuits they'll find familiar. They glance over and the object catches their eye, then he puts it away without a word. The bible, handcuffs, a yarmulke, a copy of the Quran. He doesn't have to say: *I'm Jewish like you, or Muslim like you, or Christian like you, or, wait here while I change into my leather and locate my whip.* Whatever they're into, they feel understood. They relax. They imagine the possibilities of a drop cam. The risk is in reading the household wrong. He has only a matter of minutes to collect clues before deciding which lure to use. A Bible, the Quran, a yarmulke, handcuffs. It's all about slipping them in and out of sight quickly. The wrong one could backfire, and the timing has to be right. He's made more sales than he'd ever dreamed of making. Do you remember the image that advertisers inserted into an ice cube in a glass of Scotch in the sixties? It was of a man and woman kissing. Bruce walks into a client's front hallway, from there into the living room, assessing his surroundings. Casually the seductive object slides from the darkness of his briefcase into full view, remains tantalizingly visible for no more than a second before he snatches it back. A wrong guess, an offensive choice of object, could cost him a sale or worse. He gets off on it.'

'And you're in love with this magician salesman?'

'Fallen. Utterly.'

'And him?'

'I'm not sure he takes anything seriously, not even what he loves most. When he first moved back to Australia, he exported Aboriginal art to China. His passion for the art didn't stop him from exploiting it. He bought Aboriginal designs and hired Pakistani weavers to make cushion covers, eyeglass cases, and wall hangings. I ought to loathe him. Now, here he is, hawking surveillance cameras, which I hate. Little machines designed to control and betray. He won't stay, Julia. He'll get restless, go back to Australia, or back to Milan, and I'll die of sorrow. I adore him. And how does he feel about me? You'll have to ask him, dear Julia.'

'Will you introduce me?'
'Not yet.'

Daisy

I've read it again, start to finish. There's a moment when Kamar walks into a bookstore on Bloor Street, a big, neon-bright room boasting reduced prices on new and used volumes, from paperback novels to hardcover art books. All are being offered for next to nothing. Kamar has slept fitfully. She feels that the woman who has taken her in and agreed to house her for the next six months is waiting for her to make a mistake. The woman is holding off until Kamar lets her guard down, then she'll sell her into prostitution. Kamar wants to believe that this woman's kindness is true, but as soon as she relaxes, terror slaps her awake. This woman would like her to drown in milk, the milk of kindness. Milk is being poured over her head, blinding her, so Kamar feels. She watches the woman's every gesture. Kamar smiles and attends English classes. The woman has taken her shopping for clothes. More kindness. The woman wants to ask Kamar many questions but restrains herself so as not to frighten the young refugee, so evidently troubled. Kamar senses the woman's self-restraint and wonders what other desires she's reining in and for how long the woman's self-restraint will last. Kamar's paranoia grows. The more concerned and watchful her sponsor becomes, the more endangered Kamar feels. As soon as the woman tries to sell her, Kamar will run. Kamar has a plan. She keeps a bundle of provisions on the ready, moving it nightly from one hiding place to the next inside her sponsor's house. She has no idea where to go next.

Kamar has a friend, Amira, a young woman she met in the camp in Turkey, one of the fortunate ones also offered a chance to start over in Canada. Amira now lives with her nine-year-old daughter in a small apartment near Dundas and Sherbourne, and has offered to take in Kamar. But Amira is hoping to move soon, as every time she opens her door and steps into the hallway the man from the apartment opposite opens his door to stare at her, his hands exploring between his legs. Amira worries about her daughter. They try to slip in and out of their apartment as quietly as possible. Kamar would live under a bridge rather than face such a man daily.

In the bookstore Kamar opens a volume on Middle Eastern art. She sits on the floor between the shelves, drying tears from her face with her sleeve and turning the pages, and nobody bothers her. When several minutes have passed, a young man asks, 'Are you okay?' Her nod satisfies him, and he leaves her alone. She flips from fourteenth-century Syrian ceramics to an Iranian tablecloth, a *sofreh*, onto which Nazgol Ansarinia has inscribed the prices of food sold in the streets of Tehran. The prices rise and fall the length of the finely woven cloth. On the next page, Nazgol has taken fragments of contradictory articles from newspapers, all recounting the same event, and arranged these divergent reports in a pattern that mimics the ornate use of tiny mirrors in traditional Iranian design. Kamar closes the book. From the shelf she takes a square, white volume featuring on its cover a Modernist building whose walls slope at interesting angles. The book's title names the building: *The Aga Khan Museum*. She opens the book and enters the museum. In front of her hangs a tapestry pierced by over one million golden pins. The heads of the pins, tiny gleaming dots on black cloth, and on blue where water flows, depict a formal garden, a place of repose inspired by Rumi, replete with animals and flowers. On the opposite side of the tapestry, Kamar's eyes encounter a golden forest of penetrating sharpness. Pointing straight at her are the million tips of the tightly arranged pins, which on the other side of the cloth form the garden, its blossoming plants and wild animals. *Your Way Begins on the Other Side*, she reads, and the artist's name: Aisha Khalid. Kamar sets aside the book on the Aga Khan Museum and stares at her legs leading to her feet. When a few minutes have passed and her heart is beating less wildly, she takes several more art books from the shelves and looks through them. *Theodore Bauer 1921–1986.* The desperate energy of his drawings convinces her that Bauer has seen inside her head. She must have the book. A sticker on the front announces that the price has been reduced by 60 percent, due to defects on pages 12 and 30. Also pages 35 and 36 are missing. She purchases the Bauer, emerges onto the sidewalk, is overwhelmed by noises and movement coming at her from all directions, and heads for a park, which she is quite certain she walked past earlier in the day. On a bench in the shade of a tree, she opens her new book, takes a pen from her purse, and draws on top of a painting by Bauer. She adds the words *Girl disguised as a paper kite*, then turns several pages before again drawing overtop another watercolour. *Girl growing under the earth* is the name she gives to the altered picture. She inscribes her new title in the pleasing blue ink that flows from her pen. Her other re-workings of Bauer's drawings and paintings she names: *Kamar's eyes being stolen*, *Kamar in a box*, and *My mind impersonating a field of flowers*.

Shall I, as F. H. Homsi, offer *Don't Get Me Wrong* to a small, independent publisher? F. H. Holmes is not an option. On this point Clara is unyielding. I will have to be forthright with the publisher. An advance from a publisher, made out to F. H. Homsi, would be of no use to me or to Clara. The publisher will have to be someone whose taste runs to odd books, ones in which language implodes in places, a person sufficiently peculiar and risk-prone to agree to work with me as I play stand-in for an utterly inaccessible author who insists I adopt a Syrian pseudonym. Oliver Bodinar of Gimbal Books: he, I think, is the right person.

Julia

Last night, a child's drawing woke me. I was asleep, so must have dreamed the drawing. It looked familiar. Wax crayons had been used to create a boat with a single sail. Not tilting, not propelled by wind, the boat becalmed in flat water occupied the centre of the page. A minimum number of straight lines and pale colours had been recognized as sufficient to express what mattered. I saw my sister's touch, her eye and hand. It was a drawing familiar to me from when I was small. All Clara's drawings from long ago had the same clean lines and stillness. I realized, when I woke from contemplating her picture of a motionless sailboat, that the tenderness I'd once felt for her I still felt, underneath my distrust and fear. Not all the tenderness she inspired in me had died as I'd hoped it might die.

This morning I left a note taped to her door. I did not say in the note that if she once more shot arrows at me from her tower, I would walk away forever. 'Dear Clara,' I wrote. 'Last night, I dreamed of a drawing you did as a child. It was of a sailboat, done in crayon. I liked it. The boat looked peaceful.

But that's not why I'm writing to you. Alice has fallen and fractured her shoulder. She's recovering well, in a home for seniors, where she can press a button for help and feels safe. All best, Julia.'

Clara

My sister has left me a note. 'Alice has fallen,' writes Julia. A fractured shoulder has landed Alice in an institution for seniors. She is recovering and feels much safer with a button to press, one that will bring help running to her side, day or night. I have been informed of Alice's plight, so that I cannot escape visiting Alice. Julia is once more playing the role of Alice's messenger. I feel sorry for Alice. I don't know why, but I do. It is possible that I feel affection for Alice, when conditions allow it, when Alice behaves, though I don't know for sure. If my distrust precludes affection, then what I feel is dutiful concern, nothing more. I may never know for sure what I feel for Alice.

Maurice

'Oh,' rising in his throat, 'oh, oh,' spilling out, 'oh,' and his laughter infecting every person in the room. I am jealous. Put me in your mouth and drink me, Mr. Fancy Shoes, Mr. Blue Door, Mr. Handcuffs, Mr. Yarmulke, Mr. Quran, Mr. Bible, ready as you are to seduce anyone, not just to sell surveillance cams, but for the giddy pleasure of it, anywhere, any time.

Daisy

'So, Oliver, what do you advise?'

'Hire a good lawyer. We have one we use. He could make up a contract for you both to sign, giving you power to act as F. H. Homsi and declaring the work to be Homsi's property. But is Clara Hodgkins competent to sign? Might she claim coercion later on?'

'She might not sign.'

'Then you have no choice but to give her back her work.'

'If she signs, I'm protected legally, maybe, but...'

'You don't need to do this, Daisy. I love the manuscript. I agree, it should be published. I want *Don't Get Me Wrong* to become a Gimbal book. But yes, we could find ourselves in a very uncomfortable situation.'

'Ideally, Clara signs a contract giving F. H. Homsi power to make all decisions over her manuscript, and Homsi's earnings belong to Clara, minus a small fee for me for playing the role of Homsi. In all communication with media, should media show any interest, I respond as Homsi, who refuses to make public appearances or to do interviews, except in writing.'

'We could plan a well-timed reveal. Leak the story of how the manuscript was delivered to your front porch by someone whose name we refuse to divulge. You come forward and confess to being Homsi. I defend your right to pose as a non-existent Syrian author. You defend yourself. Clara stays safe.'

'No. We don't plan to reveal anything. Homsi isn't a game. Homsi is a necessity. Here's my bigger fear: what if the book doesn't succeed as well as Clara feels it should and she takes out her anger and disappointment on herself, or it succeeds too well and she reacts who knows how?'

'It's all insane.'

'I'm willing to be Homsi.'

'I'll have our lawyer prepare two contracts, one for you to become Homsi, and another for the sale of the manuscript to Gimbal Books. Give me a bit of time to get that sorted out. Then you'll ask Clara to sign both contracts, you'll sign both, and we'll see how she responds.'

'I meet her next Thursday.'

'That's tight. I'll do my best. If you wake up tomorrow, Daisy, and have a change of heart, you do know that you can abandon this adventure? Lots of good books exist. Though none quite like this one. Damn. As soon as she's signed, we get right down to editing and release the book before one of us gets cold feet.'

Clara

I swam away from my parents' island. Many miles of water separated me from my goal: the shore of a smaller island farther out. Having to cross a large distance appealed to me, the hard fact of it. Swimming the crawl was, in my experience, no more difficult than breathing. All that was required was that I move my arms and legs in calm, steady strokes. That I swam with such ease perplexed my parents and my sister. Polyplexed, preflexed, polyglotted them, it did. I was not considered strong. The muscles that propelled me hid themselves from view. My muscles remained a mystery, which I did not fathom, could not fathom, and I attributed my swimming ability to the calm I felt when suspended in water. The inevitability of each movement performed by my legs and arms made the world logical and self-evident at last, a world willing to embrace me without demanding that I speak, without demanding that I explain. What do you need defined? I can start with your knees. Shall we move down? The queen is permitted a certain freedom of movement denied the knight. Who is your pawn? My father and a friend of his had agreed to oversee my progress. They would do so from the safety of a rowboat, into which I might climb were I to become exhausted. That was their plan. How I would find the energy to heave myself into a narrow rowboat without tipping it, were I too weak to swim, was, I suspected, a question to which neither my father nor his friend had given much thought. However, I did not intend to become too tired to swim. The boat was yellow and much valued by my father. It was made of fibreglass, modelled on the skiffs in which he'd rowed as a university student. If I could remove him from the day that I swam to that faraway island and back, I would do so. But there he is, Jack Hodgkins in his yellow boat, pleased with his skill at rowing. He braces his feet, leans in, then pulls back on the oars. I do not remember. Unwanted penetration of smiles and whispers, unassailable generations of winks and nods, highest bidder walks away with my little fists. To remember would mean death. He is a dangerous man but not as dangerous as my mother. He desires me. His desire angers him. I am the object of his anger. I am the object of their game. I seal all my orifices. Do not enter. Daily, the world would stuff itself inside me, if I let it. See not, hear not, speak not. All fornicators shall burn in hell. I am a certified virgin. Once I was well out into the bay, my mother, Alice, came down on the rocks. She stood below our cottage and aimed her binoculars at my small head, which protruded from the water. Next, she swooped her gaze from left to right until she located my potential rescuers in their rowboat. Deep in conversation, the two men had allowed the boat to angle away from me. The distance separating us was growing with every pull my father gave to the oars. Alice passed the binoculars to the wife of the man accompanying my father, this woman having expressed her desire, her fermented longing, to see the widening gap between swimmer and boat. Alice did so reluctantly, and right away asked that her spying device be handed back. I would learn of this drama only as I heaved myself out of the water onto the rocks of my parents' island, much later, having covered the distance I'd set out to conquer, a round trip from our island to the island that we stared at while eating our meals, or when we looked up from reading, while seated on the front deck, or when we raised our heads while drying on the smooth granite point. Always we stared at the same view, at the same island never the same, bright and dark dancing across it, mist swallowing it. Much of my childhood has been erased. The view of that island remains, and the sensation of swimming. How is it possible to obliterate years and years of visual, olfactory, and auditory content? *Content* being what is contained, not a feeling of contentment. I do not mean that I was contented but that I was the content of someone else's fantasy. I do remember the sensation of being caressed by water, of belonging to the water as it gathered itself into waves.

Daisy

Skin must slide over bone and muscle, if muscle is to move freely. The leg requires that I massage its long red scar. I find touching the scar odious. I prefer the pain that comes from pushing the leg to bend at the knee, forcing it hard, using my good leg to apply steady pressure. Touching the scar makes the metal beneath it real and the damaged nerves real. If I do not massage the scar several times a day, an area of fixity will establish itself, a domain of epidermal resistance will impede the leg from bending. I force myself to massage the scar. In the coming weeks, should the leg refuse to bend further than it is now capable of doing, should it fail to make progress, and should this be the result of some error on my part, or lack of will on my part, or neglect on my part, I could not forgive myself, and anger would make me want to destroy an object close at hand, anything within my reach. But past experience warns me against small acts of destruction as a route to relief. The few times I've smashed an object, hoping to dull my fury, loneliness and grief have welled up. Better to curl under my covers, shutting out as much light as possible, better to reject the outside world. Should the leg fail to progress, and its failure be due to an error or lack of will on my part, better to hide. Therefore I must exercise. I must do as I'm told, not because I believe that my obedience will result in progress and healing, but to avoid the horror of irresponsibility, of being to blame, when the hoped-for recovery does not occur. When I explained this to Ralph, he laughed and looked at me with a tenderness that made me ache. If only Ralph desired me as I do him, but he does not. Other women, yes, and never the same one for long, and always a beauty, and most often an ocean separating him from her, that is the way Ralph approximates happiness. We are friends. 'You,' says Ralph. 'There is no one like you.'

I don't know either of them well, my neighbours on the other side of the wall. Bruce, who moved in shortly before my accident, is a smart dresser with two-tone shoes and the nervous energy of a racehorse. His lover's name is Maurice. At first I resented them both. I considered selling my house, my home, despite my broken leg, to escape the noise of their orgasms. Moving from my front room to my back room proved useless. They moved with me, shrieking and moaning joyously. Morning, noon, middle of the night. But I didn't telephone with my advice, nor did I pound on the wall. When I couldn't bear it any longer, I shrieked and moaned as loudly as I could from my side of the wall. I'm quite sure they didn't hear me. Then, without warning, they quieted. I hoped they were using the upstairs rooms. I didn't want them to stop; I just didn't want to have to listen. Their cries, and gasps, and laughter made me jealous. I considered banging a hole in the wall by swinging the fibreglass carapace and the leg inside it against the plaster wall. But behind the smooth plaster the leg would have encountered brick. They grew even quieter. Let their happiness continue out of earshot – that was my wish. Silence. Now the cast is gone and I keep sliding my foot down the wall, listening, forcing the leg to bend half a degree further. Breathe, breathe, release.

The leg. Already I am dragging the leg with me from room to room; do I want to be shackled to Clara Hodgkins as well? *Don't Get Me Wrong* will win an important award. I will drown in an ocean of argument. Pressure for F. H. Homsi to appear in public will mount. His non-existence discovered, I'll be accused of fraud and of voice appropriation. *Don't Get Me Wrong* will be loved by some readers who will feel less alone in their confusion, while others will declare that the work should never have been published. They will claim that a character like Kamar suggests that all Syrian refugees suffer from mental illness and burden the Canadian state. Such critics will insist: 'Where is the virtue in creating a negative portrait of someone who has endured unimaginable hardship? This book further abuses the traumatized through stigmatization.'

But if F. H. Homsi is not uncovered? When attacked, he will refuse to defend his novel. He will ask Oliver Bodinar to do the defending. Oliver will inform the media that one need not experience years of shelling and the collapse of society for trauma to be real, and that mental illness can blossom anywhere, any time, explosive as a minefield, and without apparent cause, and that Kamar is just Kamar. F. H. will thank Bodinar.

The Girl and the Judge. This tale, dear reader, tears at Kamar.

Once, a girl was happily doing her chores, happily sweeping under the bed, when she spotted a gleaming penny and snatched it up. She hurried to the store and bought a pot of molasses, which she brought home and hid. She pursued her domestic tasks until, feeling a pang of hunger, she straightened up, stretched her tired arms, took hold of the molasses, and ate. The moment the molasses touched her tongue it revived her. The molasses made her restless and eager. Full of youthful energy, she stepped outside and skipped down the road. As soon as the girl was gone, a crow flew into the house, grabbed the pot of molasses in her beak, and left for the forest. When the girl returned home, she saw that her molasses was gone. A red-hot fury took hold of her. She set off to catch and punish the thief. Soon she spotted the crow in the distance, and guessed the bird's destination. She took a shortcut to the forest, where she ambushed the crow and cut off her tail. The crow, when she noticed that her tail was gone, attacked the girl, plucking out her eyes. Miserable and in terrible pain, the girl groped her way to the home of the village judge from whom she demanded justice.

'Your Honour, I am but a small girl, nothing more.'

'If this is what God made you, do not complain. On the contrary, be grateful for what you are.'

'I was happily doing my chores, sweeping the floor with care.'

'To do your chores may be considered an act of faith and is therefore commendable. I congratulate you.'

'A gleaming coin lay under the bed, and it caught my eye.'

'You took wise advantage of your good eyesight and luck.'

'I bought a pot of molasses.'

'You ate. You enjoyed. Good for you!'

'The rest I hid.'

'Looking forward to eating the rest later pleased you.'

'Feeling tired from my chores, I ate a bit more of the molasses, which revived me.'

'Your suffering was almost non-existent.'

'A crow flew into my house, without invitation, and stole the rest of my molasses.'

'If she'd not eaten, she might have died. The crow had been travelling, hungry to the point of exhaustion.'

'I became furious and went looking for her. When I found her, I cut off her tail. In revenge, she plucked out my eyes.'

The judge walked over to his window and looked out. When he turned to face the girl, he had an announcement to make.

'No more discussion is needed. You and the crow are even. You both have suffered and owe each other nothing.'

The judge's verdict enraged the girl. She stopped in the doorway as she was leaving and told the judge that his verdict satisfied nobody. She called him an unjust dreamer, and declared that his true place was not inside a courtroom, wielding authority, but outside, lined up with all the ordinary people. Having spoken her judgment, she left.

In both the tales that haunt Kamar, a girl is blinded. Though Kamar can't bear hearing about eyes, neither can she stop thinking about them. Blindness repulses and fascinates her. The blindness of judges and the blindness of victims. The fate of the girl in this tale makes Kamar wonder if it is justice or revenge she dreams of. To find a good judge is difficult. Better to tell no one the truth – her truth.

I have affection for crows, dear reader. Kamar feels differently. Their cawing and the beating of their wings opens trap doors in her mind. She runs across High Park, arms shielding her face. A crow can pick a person from a crowd. Scientists, funded by the U.S. Department of Defense, are studying the ability of crows to recognize individuals and to pass this information along. Of the relationship between crows and the Pentagon, Kamar learns much on the internet. Once a crow singles you out, it will remember your features for two or more years, it will tell other crows how to spot you.

Clara

Twice I've done it. Twice. I have now survived two meetings with Daisy Harding. The Daisy Harding of beautiful sentences and ingenuity. The under-recognized Daisy Harding of seven

novels, two collections of poems, and a book of essays –
volumes I've packed carefully and carted with me every time
I've moved. The Daisy Harding much taller than I expected,
with long bones, and feet buried in thick socks stuffed into
sandals. Her swollen left foot won't fit into any of her other
shoes, she felt compelled to explain. She informed me that
she wants to keep a close eye on her leg. Despite the increasingly cool weather, she therefore wears a pleated skirt made
of fabric with eyelets, a skirt that ends above her knee and
exposes the serpentine scar that reaches down.

She placed a contract on the table. I could not read it. I
looked down at the mangled words. They twisted in and out
of each other, every sentence a train wreck. 'I'll take this
home,' I told her. 'I'll read it at home.' She didn't attempt to
dissuade me.

Daisy

Without my weight pounding through them these past
months, my bones have been transforming into lace. Today,
I tried walking to the kitchen, both feet on the floor for the
first time. Every second step, the collective weight of my
head, shoulders, hips, and inner organs descended through
my pirate limb into my heel, shifted to the arch, rolled onto
the ball, and I, terrified, lowered my good foot too fast and
lurched forward. This does not pass for normal walking. I
am to request of this feeble, amnesiac leg that it hold me
upright. I am instructed, now, to welcome the vertical force
I was told to spare my bones a few weeks ago. I am ordered
to trust the leg. I am, today, to think of it as mine. This,
then, is *my* leg. Mine to teach. Mine to trust. So I am told.

Julia

My father drove off the road. He stopped the car. It was intentional, his leaving the road and entering a field of tall grass. The field belonged to him and sloped down to a brook, then climbed again. On the far slope he'd planted a forest and built a wooden platform with a roof but no walls. He'd constructed a bridge that spanned the brook. He'd also erected, before he met our mother, a tarpaper shack large enough to shelter one narrow cot and a pot-bellied stove. For a wife and two children the shack was inadequate.

As soon as he pulled off the road, he got out of the car to unlock the gate. Our names travelled through the warm air that smelled of earth and grass and blossoms. He was calling our names – mine and Clara's. We climbed out of the back seat and lowered our feet into the tangled grass depths. 'Who wants to fly?' he asked. Up we went, grasping at the rungs of the gate, pulling with our arms. He tugged the gate along with him as he strolled backwards up the hill. He'd become what he wanted to be, pulling the gate as far as the hinge, the grass, and thistles, and the height of the ground allowed. He'd become what he'd always wanted to be: a husband, a father, a custodian of sixty acres, where already he'd planted hundreds of saplings in rows. He let go.

We sailed, Clara and I, side by side, clinging to our metal wing. It swept us under the sky and down the slope, flattening the grass, disrupting insects, sending the fragrant air through my lungs in twists of delight and fear that my mouth shaped into high-pitched screams. Clara rode next to me, eyes wide open, hands and feet firm, smile exposing new, bigger-than-before teeth. In my memories of her as a child, Clara is mute. Either she spoke very little or I've erased her words. Her laughter and her radiant face, those I remember.

Clara

She wore a short, pleated skirt. It was oddly unimportant what she wore. I, who usually notice and care. Almost without fail, clothing tells me how to step around a person, the right tone, vocabulary, and speed of speech to use with that particular person dressed in that manner. Again, a short skirt despite the bite, the beautiful tiny teeth of October, the freeing from dampness. Ugly, mauve sandals over thick, striped socks – soon, she explained, she'll try to borrow a pair of boots from a male friend with large feet. The day we met I was hiding inside layers of cloth, as always. My body, disgusting to begin with, has now begun to swell. Folds of fat are forming, for which these fucking medications are to blame. No, Kevin, you won't convince me to stop taking my meds. I trick myself into believing I've concealed my belly quite cleverly, but then a window. The glassy truth: I resemble a collapsing tent. Daisy has not allowed herself to comment on my appearance, nor do her eyes linger. 'Were you able to read the contract?' she asked. 'Did you find time?' Yes, I found time! Yes, I made time! How fluidly Daisy shifts away from my oddity to time management, a common area of difficulty, hinting, in this way, that I may have something in common with other human beings. I grinned my approbation of her kindness.

'I've signed it,' I told her, and she looked pleased. More than pleased.

'Oh. How wonderful,' exclaimed Daisy.

I slid a brown envelope to her across the table. The waiter heard it slide. I could see from the corner of my eye how intently he was listening. Daisy slipped out the contract and flipped to the back page, where she saw that my signature was waiting for her to admire it.

'I am so pleased, and a bit frightened.'

'Frightened?'

'Well. I am to become F. H. Homsi and report back to you. You're fine with the percentages?'

'I've signed.'

'Yes. I just hope.'

'What is frightening you?'

'Your possible disappointment.'

'In you?'

'In me, in the book's reception.'

'It's not published yet.'

'But it will be. Oliver wants to get to work right away. He's pushing it to the top of his list. It feels a bit rushed but I think we should go with his timing. Your book is to come out as soon as possible. Within a year, stores will be carrying it.'

'You're F. H. Homsi. You decide.'

'And you'll go along.'

'I won't. I don't go along. But I do let things go by. I'll look the other way, so I'm not tempted to stop you.'

'Now is your chance to back out. We can tear up the contract.'

'I'd better go. I'm leaving now. Thank you, Daisy. I've paid for my coffee. Good luck.'

It was gliding upwards, the voice elevator in its dark shaft. I felt Bridgette and Kevin and the others ascending. When they reached my head, they'd all get off. My head was their favourite floor. They'd pour out of their glass tube. I'd try to confine them. They'd shove their way out, shouting over one another, testing to see who could convince me the fastest to slit my wrists.

I made it out of the stuffy café into the cold air and started walking. Quickly a rhythm asserted itself and carried me along. In the voice elevator, jammed between floors, Kevin and the others continued abusing each other. I plunged deeper into the cold air, felt the wonder of it against my skin. Bridgette, of course, was crying and moaning. Thanks to the cold air and the brisk pace imposed by my legs, her distress arrived muffled, and Kevin's threats translated into nothing more than a persistent pain in the arch of my right foot. Oh, glorious, cold air.

Maurice

Trust him? I do.

Julia

Clara has responded to my note about Alice. A visit to Alice from Clara may soon be possible. All depends on how Clara, on what Clara. All depends on Clara's ability to hold Clara in one piece.

I am once more looking through the box of books I saved from her basement apartment when she moved. She asked me to deliver it, and a dozen like it, to the dump, and I agreed. 'Please dispose of all the boxes, thank you. Get rid of them whatever way you like, so long as I never have to see them again!' On the very top lay a picture book I recognized. I lifted it out. The price of looking is that once you've seen, you've seen. For thousands of years we've warned each other not to look.

Raggedy Ann Stories by Johnny Gruelle. 1918 edition. Slender volume, broken spine, coloured plates.

Our mother's name is inscribed in pencil, followed by her childhood address. The illustration on the front cover shows Raggedy Ann, a cloth doll. She is wearing a flowered dress, a white apron, and she sits propped against a blackboard. Unquestioning happiness is stitched on her round face. Two big black buttons are her marvelling eyes. On the back cover, she's turned her back to the reader. Right arm raised, rag in hand, she has just erased the blackboard, and perhaps the words of her own story?

Next comes a gutted book. No legible title. This is one of Clara's creations. On the front, a face: abject suffering sculpted from shiny layers of black and brown pigment, nose protruding and lips contorted. On the back, rough strokes produce another face: blurred rush of anger and fear. Down the book's spine the white rungs of a ladder.

The day I first looked through this box and decided to keep it, I couldn't stop myself. Untrue. I could have stopped but chose not to. I reached in, pulled out the next volume. *Pinocchio: The Story of a Puppet by Collodi.* (Carlo Lorenzini.) Edited and illustrated by Violet Moore Higgins. A Just Right Book. Albert Whitman & Company Publishers, Chicago, U.S.A. 1927.

Cover: dark green with gold lettering. A picture in red and white presents the hero. Balancing on his right foot, he attempts to free his left leg from a hole in a heavy door, a hole he's created by thrusting his left foot through the wood. Now, grasping his shin with both hands, he leans backwards and tugs, determined to release his imprisoned limb, an expression of dismay spreading across his face.

Violet Moore Higgins has permitted herself three colours (black, white, red), and her drawings are distributed with economy. A quotation from the text accompanies each picture.

One by one, that first day, I removed and examined each book:

Etymological Dictionary of the English Language.

Oxford University Press. 1978. (first edition 1879–1882)

I allowed it to fall open of its own accord. 'Apple: the fruit of the apple-tree. The apple of the eye is properly the pupil; but was sometimes used of the eye-ball, from its round shape.' Page 27.

A pleasing pink paperback, titled *The World within the Word: Essays by William H. Gass.* Published in 1976 by Basic Books, a member of Perseus Books Group.

I turned to the opening essay, 'The Doomed and Their Sinking.' It offered the following statement, which struck me as true and therefore delighted me: 'the crazy can garrote themselves with a length of breath, their thoughts are open razors, their eyes go off like guns.' Page 4.

At the very bottom of the box lay a book boasting 147 colour plates. *Theodore Bauer: Works on Paper.* Prestel Verlag. München. 1979.

On the front, a brusque watercolour of a tulip; petals like fence pickets, seven in number and slender.

I flipped it open. Plate 3. In black pen, in Clara's distinct, surprisingly round and open handwriting: *Girl who claims to be a paper boat.*

Plate 4. Rapid strokes of Bauer's brush suggest wildflowers ruffled by wind, and more wind moving through grass. Clara's added, *I am trying unsuccessfully to become a field of flowers.*

Plate 7. Collaged strips of paper, two indistinct grey shapes side by side. Clara has renamed them: *Girl whose face is torn. My features have been reduced to two hazy birds, pecking.*

Plate 8. The same tulips as on the front cover. Beneath the erect petals, Clara's declared: *My hand reaches up for help.*

Plate 17. What appears to have been a painting of two tin cans, balanced, one on top of the other. Clara has outlined three pale patches, turning these into eyes and a mouth: *Little Girl.*

Plate 18. An area of red paint resembles an open mouth in profile. Teeth have been added and the words *Little Girl Screaming.*

The first time I opened Clara's copy of *Theodore Bauer: Works on Paper*, I revisited each plate more than once, counting petals, counting birds, the nightmare interior of Clara's mind pressing close. I looked for patterns. Doing so calmed me. This seeking of patterns, doubtless, is what she does continuously, to survive.

Maurice

We laugh. He trips again. He flings himself with abandon. His performed awkwardness frees me. The burden of opinion, a weight I've carried all my life, is lifted as I watch his legs and arms fly through the air, uncensored. As far back as I can remember, my own gaze has crushed me. The gorgeous Bruce Mammadov tosses his arm, his leg, into space, trusting. Not trusting that he won't fall but that he will fall. He'll laugh, and again let go. He'll throw himself into the centre of the room, or down the street, or into the river, or through the nettles, or along the rocky path, or into the fountain, or into someone's arms. Sounds rush out of him, the world pours in. I gaze. From the weight of judgment he removes all weight. As if uncorking champagne, he presses his delightful thumbs into the evil neck of hierarchy and sends all unkind assessments flying across the room. All my life I have feared the eyes of others fixed upon me, and equally feared that without their gaze I would cease to exist. The best way to explain is to tell you the story of the dog and his bowl.

Simon the basset hound belonged to a friend. I offered to take care of him for thirty days, while his owner went wandering about Brazil. For thirty days I accepted full responsibility for Simon's four stubby legs, his flapping ears and dangling tongue, his inquisitive nose and apologetic tail. I became answerable for the well-being of the smooth-haired brown-and-white length of him. I filled his bowl with food and placed it on the floor. I'd been instructed to watch him eat. 'If you don't, he'll starve,' my friend had warned me. While Simon slurped and chewed, I sat on a kitchen stool and bore witness. But curiosity got the better of me. What would happen if I walked away? I did so and the hum of the refrigerator replaced the crunch and suction of food being consumed by a drooling mouth. Simon had turned his back on his bowl. He refused to eat. As soon as I resumed my perch and stared in his direction, he once more attended to the task of feeding himself, and did so with audible passion. A wave of nausea rose in me. I realized what Simon and I had in common: a desperate desire for permission. That I craved solitude suggested an independence I did not possess. I isolated myself so as not to feel the intensity of my need for approval. To breathe, to eat, to think my own thoughts – I was a grown man who sought permission to perform these fundamental acts. To so desire permission and approval, to see my desperate needs mirrored in the behaviour of a neurotic dog, inspired horror in me. At the end of thirty days, I returned Simon to his owner with immense relief.

The era of the neurotic dog is the era in which we live. Dogs riding in strollers, a dog seated on a folding chair placed in the shade of a tree. As for me, I've made my body a place of discipline. Two hours minimum at the gym three times a week. Julia mocks me. I've not seen Julia in weeks. Julia, who has known me for decades. I roll over in bed and gaze at Bruce, at his closed eyes, the delicate lids of skin concealing the damp surface of those shifting orbs. Dreams are tightening and loosening his breath. I watch it escape from between his lips.

'Bruce?'

'I was dreaming. Can you scratch, just down there, yes, yes, no, yes, an inch lower, aaah, yes, aah, good, good, very good.'

'Will you come flying in the ultralight, if there's no wind, later today?'

'No.'

'Because?'

'I don't want to fall out of the sky.'

'Is it my flying you don't trust, or my building skills? I check every nut, screw, wire, and rod, every connection, before taking off, always, every time.'

To silence me he positioned his mouth so that it covered mine, and his tongue searched for home.

Daisy

Now that it plays a constructive part, now that it has become a contributing member, bearing a portion of my weight, with gratitude I accept it as *mine* from here on in. True, I have cause for pointless resentment. My leg has stolen possibilities from me, and that's not all: it has altered my character.

Pleasure, however, it gives – the dense, hard, satisfaction of the arduous, of the deliberate and well-performed. When my left foot, in its black sock, slides down the wall in tiny jerks, I watch with the avid eye of a card shark to see if I'm winning. If my toe descends below the white dot of exposed plaster, where the red paint has been chipped from the wall, then I win; if not, the white dot of plaster wins. I force my left ankle and foot downward, until the muscles of my thigh scream that they can stretch no further, and the knee joint squeals, and the leg will not bend further. No matter, further, further, breathing hard and slow. Ahhh, but what's this? My foot is gaining territory, inch by inch, parting the red sea (a terrible colour to have painted a dining room – what was I thinking all those years ago?). Every inch gained is the result of pressure applied from above, applied by the heel of my good foot upon the ankle of my unwilling-to-bend leg. Through the wall I hear my neighbours laughing. Over and under each other, their amusement flows. A stream of delight sparkles on the far side of the brick wall that separates my rooms from theirs. They are in love. Bruce and Maurice. The sound of their orgasms moves from the front room to the back room to the front room. They argue about one subject only: surveillance cameras. Bruce sells them. Maurice disapproves. Once more they're going at it, amicable, sly, persistent.

'Tiny, perfect ones for home use? What am I doing here? You're not oblivious, just immoral. Distrust. It spreads, you know. Social gangrene, intimate amputations, that's what parents surveying their kids leads to, and lovers filming lovers, everyone spying on each other.'

'Maurice, Maurice. I'm going to install a camera in the living room. I'll lie on the sofa repeating your name, while the camera records my devotion. We've all been performing forever. A camera records. Tell them you're installing it and where, that's my advice to clients. Use it to create fellow feeling, clown about. A camera can be put to any number of uses.'

'Sure, document little Johnny kicking his sister, catch Nancy spilling her milk and the nanny yelling. That'll make for an easier day in court.'

'Some love the attention, others don't.'

'Proof over privacy.'

'Did I show you the footage, from yesterday, of you in the shower?'

'Bruce.'

'Yes, Maurice?'

'Not funny.'

'I'll never forget the day we met. You knocked on my door. I opened it. You confessed that you'd been spying on me for weeks, that I'd become part of an exhibit in an art gallery across the street. You and who knows how many others had been watching me through binoculars.'

'Not the same. Nothing was recorded.'

Daily, their arguments and tender reconciliations drift through the wall as my left foot, in its black sock, inches downward, past the chip in the paint, approaches the pencil line, then stops and will go no further. The knee joint locks in anguish, the quadricep remains too tight, the foot in its black sock descends no further.

Clara

Kamar is gone. I've given her away. For once, Bridgette is smiling. Her competitor is gone. 'Smiling like an idiot doesn't stop your nose running,' says Kevin under his breath. He's watching me closely. 'You'll find out soon enough,' he hisses in my ear. 'You'll find out what they do with your Kamar. Use her to wipe the coffee stain off their desk.' I must keep walking. There's the white elephant. The yard is small. The elephant leaves room for nothing else. What is the elephant made of? I've never dared reach out and touch it. I could. I could run my fingers along its trunk or down its immense flank, but someone would be watching from the window. Metal fencing keeps the elephant in. The pachyderm is packed into the yard. They must slip the lawn mower beneath it. They've mowed, so somehow got under the belly of the beast. Neither snow nor ice has reduced the animal. From one winter to the next it survives. It stands in its yard. The owners of the house cannot bring themselves to part with their artwork. Perhaps they love it. Perhaps they argue with each other regarding the future of the elephant that is consuming such a large portion of their property. It towers next to me as I walk by. At Christie Street I stick out my arm. With my other hand I press the button commanding the yellow sign to illuminate itself. Suspended midway across the street, the flashing sign announces my presence, and that I intend to make an attempt to reach the other side. I look both ways and wait for the cars to stop. Arm extended, I step forward. I like to make them stop. Last week Kevin whispered, 'Do it again,' so I turned the moment I reached the other side and crossed back to where I'd come from. 'Again,' he giggled. Kevin doesn't often giggle. As I embarked on my third crossing, a driver honked, another yelled through their window: 'What's wrong with you? Make up your fucking mind!' At the sound of yelling, Bridgette burst into tears. Kevin started glee-snorting, choking on his own delight, scraping wax from his ear and sucking the wax from the tip of his finger. When he gets excited he indulges in his worst habits. I was running now, and raced the length of a block. I wouldn't have slowed down, but the cramp in my side got worse. I came to the elementary school where the children are kept out at lunchtime, but also kept in, the yard fenced. The children move about in clusters, smaller formations breaking off, forming new chemical compounds. A few lone atoms were drifting, over there, under the solitary tree. Beside the fence, two were digging a hole. They were planning their escape. Kamar escaped from several camps. I went online and stared at pictures of those places. It was one of Kamar's former homes and consisted of row upon row of canvas tents. First the sun beat down, then the sky split open and water pummelled the tents and the dirt road and the dirt between the tents. An outhouse existed, somewhere, likely overflowing with urine and feces. One bucket per how many? It wasn't the camp that scared me but the internoose, pretending to open while tightening around everything. On the internoose I listened to the camp's cacophony of grief and hunger, its dust and shit scuffle, a curse concert of decomposing lives. Before handing Kamar over to Daisy Harding, first I freed her from a Turkish refugee camp, jerked her across borders, murdered the man who'd raped her (I couldn't resist), tossed her into a truck, flew her across an ocean, and deposited her in a carpeted bedroom with a view of a garden. I think that's what I did with her. I meant to. 'Can't even remember where you put her?' sniggers Kevin. 'And you call yourself an author.' I plugged my ears and hummed as I walked. I did know, I did. I was the author and I decided. She lived for several months in the home of a well-meaning professor. Dr. Lydia Benjamin, geophysicist. I gave her to Lydia and her dentist husband, Max Howl. A quiet Toronto neighbourhood, that's where I made Kamar's mind come apart. It starts catching on things, small things.

Her reasoning unravels. She creates a new reasoning. Her sense of proportion vanishes. Amplification chases her down the street. She perches on the tongue of a hospital, and the hospital gulps her down. In the belly of the hospital she meets a young woman her own age, Babuk Sassani, born in Canada to Iranian parents. Babuk has chosen suicide to escape her family, whose collective attention centres on her brother. They choose not to see what sort of attention her brother focuses on her. I didn't give a name to Babuk's cherished brother as he was beneath naming. ''Cause you're scared of him,' snorts Kevin. 'She's not not not,' stammers Bridgette, chewing on the tips of her braids. 'Clara's not, not, not afraid, nobody's afraid of you, Kevin bumbum.' 'Be quiet, all of you,' I yell through my fingers, my hands covering my face. 'Shut the fuck up or I'll take away your names! I'll do to you what Julia, my devil sister, does to me. All my life I've been mistaken for Julia. Only as Julia can I talk with other people. When I'm Julia, the rest of you scuttle away in fear. I will become Julia, Queen of Volubility, Her Histrionic Self. You'd better behave or Julia will evict you. She'll tell the landlord all about you, then out we'll all go. Bump, bump, bump down the stairs.' I allow gestures of friendship between Kamar and Babuk, moments of trust. Then comes the End. I'm allowed to end it. They want me to. They want an ending, since a book needs to finish. I'm not Kamar, but we are close in our mutual inability to be close. Kevin, Bridgette, and the others are colonizers. I never invited them in. Before I sold Kamar to Oliver Bodinar, no, NO. Precision must prevail: I gave her to Daisy, SHE sold Kamar because I told her to (just as my mother sold me). There, in any case. Kevin snuck along the corridor and spat through the keyhole. I plugged it with Kleenex. Plug the hole. All holes must be plugged immediately. That made Bridgette wail and kick. I put in my earbuds

and let the Grateful Dead erect their raucous wall. I've sold
Kamar, and all I have left is language and the urge to tweezer
it apart, as if it were a clock.

Julia

The moment she saw me she waved. There she was, coming
down the street, carrying herself very straight as always.
Rows of safety pins advanced in an elegant script across
the shimmering cloth spread over her thigh. The pins
descended the skirt that rippled around her ankles. This
time she was not dressed in black (except for her sweater,
which I hoped was warm enough) but in layers of blue and
green, of net draped over silk. Her inimitable style, her
striking disguise.

'Hello.'

Eyes and mouth smiling, face radiant, there she stood, in
front of me, taking great gulps of air.

'Hello,' she repeated. 'I have to catch my breath. How are
you?'

'Fine. I'm fine, I think.'

'You're not sure?' she asked, holding herself even more
alert, her expression now quizzical.

'No, no. Fine. I'm sure, I'm fine.'

'I'd like to go visit Alice.'

'You would?'

'I can do it now, if you'll go with me. I couldn't before.
But I'm feeling well at the moment. I still couldn't go there
on my own. But if you'd come?'

'Of course.'

'I'm sorry. I know how busy you are.'

'No, no. I mean, I am busy, yes, but yes, I'd like to go with you to see Alice. When shall we go?'

'Tomorrow? Any time you like. But sooner would be better. I don't know how long this will last, this feeling good and able.'

'I can't tomorrow, but I'll come knock on your door, Friday at eleven-thirty?'

'Yes. Good. Eleven-thirty will give me time to prepare. Good. See you in three days' time, on Friday.'

Daisy

The large muscles have taken over. This was how she, the physiotherapist, explained it to me. I was lying on a mat on the floor, sliding my foot down the wall of the clinic, replicating what I do at home. 'You are cheating,' she told me. 'Your hip is shifting to allow your foot to slide lower. Your hip is obstructing your progress. Relax your arms,' she instructed. My arms relaxed. My hip had no interest in anyone's authority but its own.

She told me to kneel. Fear prevented me. She repeated her instructions and I attempted. Holding on to the bed, as she'd warned me to do, saved me from falling on my face. I pictured, in front of me, the entrance to a tent and imagined crawling inside, spreading out my sleeping bag, choosing how to position myself, the rock uneven beneath me. But crawling was impossible. I could not advance on my knees. An internal blister of self-pity burst. Sorrow trickled down my face. To hide my shame, I turned my face away from the physiotherapist. 'You're doing it,' she told me, 'you're kneeling.' I was not kneeling. Had I let go of the bed, the floor would have rushed up. 'You can do it,' she repeated. 'Good. Now do it again. See?' she asked. 'See how well you got down onto the floor?' All I could see was the entrance to a tent. All I could feel was my stiff leg pitching me forward as I clutched at the bed.

Clara

I put in my earbuds and Arcade Fire did their best to stop Kevin, but they weren't quick enough. He slipped his words in, slid them through the music wall: 'You sure fucked up big time on the bus. They'll be coming for you next. The dentist makes everyone pay. When did you last sit in the chair? Open wide. Tell me when it hurts. In he'll reach, revving up the drill. Dental work, mental work. They'll be reporting you next. Here's one who needs taking care of. Better keep your mouth shut. No more sucking on other people's beeswax. Rots your teeth. Serves you right.'

I wrote his name in large letters. He hates when I do that. *Kevin, Kevin, Kevin.* Spread out the pages on the floor. Maximum exposure. Annabelle passed me her crayons. I used a whole pad of construction paper. Some of the paper I covered in thick layers of crayon. Then I dug out his name with my fingernails. KEVIN. I liked the feeling of the wax under my nails. He was quieting, barely mumbling his vicious taunts, keeping them down his throat, where they belong, then Anabelle saw how stubby her crayons looked, I'd used so much and pressed so hard, and she started snivelling, so Kevin leaned right over and whispered in her ear, 'That's what you get, blubberhead, for lending Clara your crayons.' Then he kicked her in the shins. I couldn't shut them out or shut them in, tried walking in circles, cutting them in, cutting them out, going in circles, fists in my ears, when I saw the library book on my kitchen counter.

Syrian Folk Tales from the Hearth. I'd brought it home ages ago. I always return my books on time but this one I purposely lost and paid for. Kamar needed it. I put it in my bag and that's how Kamar was born. I took it because of the women on the bus. Open wide. They were seated right behind me, not the least interested in me, all absorbed in planning for their refugees, collecting shoes, collecting coats, hoping for a family soon. I searched my bag for my earbuds but couldn't find them, must have left them at home, like an idiot. I tried humming under my breath to shut the women out, but they were loud. Yelling might have drowned them out, but I do not yell in public. To yell in public is demeaning and makes me feel like shit. The two of them were really getting off on describing teeth. Teeth of refugee children, teeth of refugee parents, and the rot between, and the dying nerves, and bleeding gums, and I pushed my way to the doors and rang the bell but not too many times, though probably I did ring it several times, because someone did say something to me, so I pulled my hat down over my ears. Then the bus stopped. Thank God, it stopped.

I walked and walked, the rest of the way to the library. There it was, lying in the photocopier when I opened the lid. Someone had forgotten and was maybe coming back, but I took it anyhow. *Syrian Folk Tales from the Hearth*. I meant to tear it up when I got home. No more Syria, no more dentists strapping people into chairs. I'd tell the library, 'I've lost an item and am prepared to pay,' then rip the book to shreds.

Kamar didn't exist, not yet. But the girl who gouges out her eye when everyone else is spilling the beans and breaking their horns, and the girl who's blinded by the crow, they've existed forever, the ones who can't be cured. By the time I arrived at Dr. Burns's office I couldn't explain. I had the book with me but I wouldn't show it to her. *Syrian Folk Tales from the Hearth*. Every time I started to take it out of my bag I burst into tears. I sat there, sobbing, and then my hour was up. 'How will you get home?' she asked. 'I'll walk,' I told her. 'I'm not taking the bus. I refuse to take the bus. I'll consider taking public transport another day.'

I walked, and by the time I got home, Kamar had begun, and so long as I kept my mouth shut, nobody could take her from me, not even Dr. Burns, and Kamar wasn't going to get caught in a novel, she was going to be poetry until I opened my mouth and Dr. Burns wanted her to become a novel. I began to imagine I could be like other people. So I walked out my door and left Kamar on Daisy Harding's front porch. I betrayed her without Kevin or anyone else telling me to.

Julia

A parrot named Caesar. He is handsome and often hangs upside down from the bars of his cage. Bold, in his plumage of indigo, orange, and emerald, he fixes his round, unnerving eye on any person who approaches.

Alice and I discovered him in the sunroom off the lounge. I feel better about her decision to stay at St. Rita's Residence for Seniors, now that she can visit Caesar. 'For now, you are here, for now. Later we'll see,' I tell her, though she doesn't complain. I have her on waiting lists for several places. 'There will be people you know at Cavendish Gardens. When a room becomes free, they'll call us. For now, you have Caesar.

You sound happy enough. Or are you just being brave?' Alice assures me she's not just being brave. Caesar struts and eyes us with interest. Alice and Caesar, both are caged. For now, Alice has a room on the eleventh floor, facing south, into blinding sunlight except on overcast days. She has curtains made of a fabric she likes. She pulls them across the window to keep out the glare. The window overlooks a miniature world of rooftops and trees that ends in a taut line of lake, blue or silver, depending on the hour and the weather. Neither my eyes nor Alice's can see beyond the water. Neither her gaze nor mine can slip between the lake and the sky pressing down.

Alice observes the world as if she were swimming through thick milk. To have the cataracts removed from her eyes – this idea frightens her. She chooses to swim through milk rather than undergo routine surgery. The choice is hers. I cannot say what I will do when my turn comes. We have met with the surgeon, who agrees that the choice is hers alone to make. She is wheeled, thrice daily, out of her room with its milky view, and along a narrow corridor to the cramped elevator in which she rides down for meals, which she eats in a dining room with large windows at one end, square tables under pink tablecloths, and from all directions the shouting of the disturbed. Colourless food has become an inescapable feature of her days. Some of the diners prove capable of coherent conversation. Others stare mutely at their plates. Someone is cursing at this very moment, 'Goddamn sonuvabitch,' in response to which Amanda Alderson yells, 'Amanda Alderson wants her ice cream now. Please bring Amanda Alderson her dessert at once.'

This morning, while seated in her wheelchair, waiting for the elevator, Amanda kicked the buttocks of the caregiver standing in front of her.

'Amanda, please don't kick me. You must not kick me or anyone else. Please, try to be polite,' instructed the caregiver, to which Amanda retorted, 'You be polite. You try behaving for a change. If you can't behave, I'll kick you again.'

After lunch, once a week, a pianist plays popular songs on the upright piano beside the fish tank. She encourages residents to sing along. 'She's pleasant,' says Alice. 'I mouth the words. I've never been able to carry a tune, as you know. And how are you, Julia? Tell me about Julia.'

'I spoke with Clara. She's coming to see you tomorrow.'

'She is?'

'Yes.'

'How wonderful that will be. Clara and Julia together.'

'Yes, both your daughters and you. The three of us together.'

'Tell me about Julia.'

'There's not much to tell. Shall we go see Caesar?'

'Sure. Why not.'

'While we're visiting with Caesar, I'll tell you about Julia.'

'Good. I'll like that. And it's true that Clara will come tomorrow?'

'Yes, she'll come. She's said that she will. And you must not mention your cataracts.'

Maurice

He has agreed to fly. Bruce will leave the earth with me, tomorrow. We'll both be strapped in, buttocks nestled in our plastic seats, surrounded by air, propeller whirring, and gasoline sloshing behind our heads. Up, up, and slowly away. No wind. There can be no wind, or we must not fly.

Julia

Should I have not stepped inside? I knocked. She opened the door. She said she'd be ready in a moment, and she began to close the door, then hesitated. She asked, 'Do you want to come in?'

'Sure,' I answered.

From the front hall I saw that she'd painted words on the walls of the living room. *See not, speak not. Death to the Profligate.* A bird had been roughly brushed into existence in black paint, its beak held shut by an X. To the right of the unusable fireplace she'd painted a faceless pink child wearing a checkered pinafore dress and clutching a string tied to a heart-shaped balloon with *I am dead* written on it.

Her living room had become her studio – everywhere sculptures made from scraps of metal and wire. She'd knitted covers, slipped them over the sleeves of LPs, left an oval or sometimes a square opening in the woollen surface. Through this hole the singer peered out. She'd chosen only albums with photos of singers on the sleeve.

In a matter of minutes Clara returned from her bedroom at the back of her apartment. She was ready to go out. She locked the door behind us.

'Your living room,' I said. 'It's wonderful.'

'Oh.' She smiled. 'Thanks.'

We waited for the bus. As we rode in the bus, I remembered being carried by buses and streetcars to school. Because we were two, because I was not alone but accompanied by my older sister, our parents considered it safe for us to travel on our own. Together we'd walk to the bus stop. What we spoke about, I don't remember. The weight of the books on my back, the straps cutting into my shoulders – that sensation I can retrieve. Already we were leading separate lives. I knew who Clara's friends were but they were too old to be my friends. If I was seven, she was ten. How old were we? I neither knew nor asked what went on in her school world. Surviving in the classroom in which I was imprisoned all day, every day but Saturday and Sunday, week after week, consumed me. Evenings at home, we rediscovered each other. So that we could play hopscotch in the living room, we drew on the carpet with chalk. We drew giant faces, numbered the forehead, eyes, ears, nose, and mouth. We hopped from feature to feature. Our father raised a questioning eyebrow, our mother declared that the carpet was old and our artistic freedom was what mattered. But as we walked to the bus in the morning, school looming, we retreated into our separate, anxious worlds.

All institutions unnerve Clara. We arrived at St. Rita's, signed in, rode up in the elevator. Alice was waiting, perched on the edge of her bed. Clara admired Alice's necklace, Alice's haircut, Alice's good health. 'What a wonderful view,' she exclaimed, and Alice looked very pleased, and we all stood gazing out Alice's window. We saw the strip of lake beneath the pale sky, and the many rooftops, and towers, and tops of trees separating us from the edge of the world. After we'd looked at the view, Clara wheeled Alice, our mother, hers as much as mine, along the corridor to the elevator, and we all three rode down.

Caesar was waiting. We watched him hop excitedly from left to right on his swinging bar, the one suspended in the middle of his cage. We urged him to speak. We told him how much we admired his plumage and his bold demeanour.

Minutes passed.

'Caesar, Caesar. Oh, such a handsome fellow you are,' declared Alice.

'Caesar,' I tried, 'tkkkk, cackcackcack. Hey, gorgeous. Tkkktkttk.'

'You are stunning,' Clara told Caesar. 'Crawwwkcrrrrkkk.'

'Well, not today. He's not in the mood,' concluded Alice.

'You never know,' corrected Clara.

'Hey, Caesar, tkkk, cackcackackk. Hey, handsome,' I urged.

'He won't perform on command,' said Alice. 'Who likes to be told what to do?'

Clara, who'd wandered a short distance away, now returned holding a fat snowman about five inches tall, made of white, plush. It had an orange nose and belonged to a family of toy snowmen arranged prematurely along the window ledge, in festive anticipation of December, a month when snow used to fall and accumulate. One of the snowmen was playing a small, stuffed piano, two were singing, another sweeping for the sake of sweeping. Clara held up her snowman for Caesar to examine. He hopped to and fro, in a crescendo of agitation.

'Oh, so you like that?' she asked, and poked the snowman's nose between the bars, then pulled it back, just as Caesar's beak lunged. She poked it in again, out, in, out, in. His agitation mounting, Caesar hopped right, left, right.

'I love you,' he screeched. 'I love, I love you.'

Clara laughed and laughed. Alice watched and smiled.

'He knows that he's handsome,' said Alice.

'I love you, I love you,' insisted Caesar.

'I love you, I love you,' declared Clara.

Clara

I have survived seeing Alice. She's become less dangerous. But I must remain vigilant, as she is sly. I wheeled her down the hall. I pushed and she rode. That was a good move. My mistake came earlier. Before we went to visit Alice, I let Julia in. I hadn't intended to let her in. She knocked. I invited her in. She saw. Not everything, only the smallest amount. I didn't want her to comment but she did. No, that's not true. I wanted her to comment and she did. Both are true, did and didn't. 'Your living room, it's wonderful.' I felt happiness. *I can do this*, I thought.

Wonderful living room, I recited, just now, as an evening treat, as comfort food. Right away Kevin snickered. His meanest, tightest, most staccato laugh, which he reserves for occasions when he senses my vulnerability and knows that he can sneer me into obedience. 'Fine,' I told him, 'I won't let her in next time, have it your way.' This made Bridgette start spinning in circles, tears and snot running down her cheeks, and in between gulps of these fluids, she kept calling out to anyone who might have been listening: 'Kevin is picking on Clara, Kevin's being mean to Clara, Kevin is a bully,' which only caused Kevin to sharpen the blade of his snicker and drive it deeper between my ribs, until I promised not to open the door to anybody, not ever. 'Let her in again,' Kevin warned, his lips worming all over my ear, 'and she'll find out we exist, and you know what will happen then, don't you? Sure you do. She'll kill us. All of us. Bridgette first. She'll stuff B's snotty nose rag down her throat till she chokes. Then Gillian. Gilllian will really get it up the ass. You know what she'll shove inside Gillian?' He won't shut up, not until I'm screaming so loudly that I have to stick my head under my pillow or stuff clothes in my mouth, so the people in the apartment upstairs won't hear and come and knock on my door, because if they did that, if they knocked, or called the cops and the cops knocked, if anyone knocked now, I'd have no choice. But nobody's knocking, and writing this down is quieting Kevin; the written word scares him. He clams up when I expose him on paper.

Daisy

My heel stopped, inches above the pencilled line. With my right ankle I pressed down on the left ankle. Slowly, almost imperceptibly, the left foot slid, causing pain to spread from hip to knee, inside knee, down back of leg. Breathe.

I will have to paint over the path my feet have made on the dining room wall. The leg is bending. Repeat: the leg is bending better than last week. Repeat. Breathe.

I hear Maurice's voice slipping through the wall, distraught.

'Please, Bruce. Say something?'

My heel slides then jitters, passes below the pencil line, sinks further than a moment ago. Hold. Hold. Release.

'Bruce, if you won't talk, you'll never be free of this. Fine. Okay. Freedom is a bit too much to ask for. But don't go mute on me. I miss you. Please don't leave me out here, alone. I'm not coping well either. We were in it together. We were both beside her when she died. It certainly wasn't your fault. It was mine, if anyone's. My fault. Does that make me a murderer? If I'd not been so stupid, she'd be alive. That's what you're thinking, isn't it? I killed her. You needn't open your mouth. Your silence says plenty.'

I stopped sliding my foot. Maurice lowered his voice to a whisper, or perhaps he stopped speaking. I lay on my back, wondering what catastrophe had occurred.

Clara

I've signed away my rights. F. H. Homsi will approve or disallow all editorial changes. Daisy would give me back my rights, if I were to ask. I'm quite sure she would. But then I'd have to deal with Oliver Bodinar directly. I'd have to read his editorial notes, and I'd want to kill him. It's better this way. I'll never read the published text. I've given Kamar up for adoption, that's what I have to keep reminding myself. I could have aborted her, but I wanted her to live. *Don't Get Me Wrong* is the only coherent work I've ever produced and there won't be another. I had to become Julia in order to write with a reader in mind, a reader eager to be told a story, and that's not an experience I want to repeat. Dr. Burns told me to try. Dr. Burns who knows nothing, Dr. Burns insisted that I attempt coherent prose. Her Cleverness longs to pry my secrets out of me, delving with her psycho-tweezers. Dr. Burns also suggests that I try to socialize, that I attend a support group for the insane, with whom I have nothing in common but my insanity and with whom I'm therefore destined to become fast friends. What a load of shit. Insist, insist, she can be so fucking insistent, Dr. Burns can be; and so I caved and wrote a goddamn novel, to shut her up. At first it was just to shut her up. Then Kamar refused to go back where she'd come from. I had to continue writing for her sake. But now Kamar's as good as dead. Mr. Oliver Bodinar, editor, amputator of words, passage inflator, flatulent master of a tiny press nobody's heard of but Daisy, he has adopted Kamar. Adopt! Such euphemistic cowardice, you little bitch, you sold her. I've accepted money in exchange for her life. I'm a shit. Kevin's right. I'm a piece of shit and should be forced to swallow myself. I'm also free of Kamar, free now to mess with language any way I please. Dr. Burns will have no purchase. If she asks me to be coherent, I'll tell her: buy a copy of the goddamned book you forced me to write. 'You'll be sorry,' Kevin's hissing. 'Ha, ha. They'll turn your stupid book into a porn flick.' I can feel his mouth, hot against my ear. I've got to see Dr. Burns. I won't last. Not with Kevin drooling in triumph, filling my head with his slime. I'll email Dr. Burns right away. I'll go to the library, sign up for the internoose, stick my head in and press send. She'll fit me in for an extra session. I'll promise to fit in, she'll extra me in, I'll make it CLEAR. SHE MUST SEE ME, no half measures, no excuses.

Julia

'Please, Maurice.'

'She's dead and it's my fault.'

'It is not your fault.'

'Picture this carefully, Julia. The sky is blue and smooth. One field ends, next comes a width of woods, a second field slides slowly beneath us, and we pass above a country road, a row of houses, a restaurant, a gas station, the next field is bordered by maples that are brilliant yellow. I turned to look at Bruce but his head was bent. He was gazing at something below. The next field dipped, the water wasn't wide, a ribbon of darkness gone, and more trees climbed the rising slope, and next came a fenced area with horses. No, there must have been more before the horses, more fields and a few more roads. But the horses were below us when the engine cut out. I aimed for the nearest field without animals, and large enough. What Bruce was thinking, I don't know. I didn't turn to look at his face. Through the muffle of my helmet I heard him shout something, but I didn't answer. It was taking all my concentration to get us down. At the end of the field stood a bungalow, and to the left of that a barn, and because of the long, narrow shape of the field, woods on one side, a slope tumbling into marsh on the other, I had no choice but to aim for the bungalow, hoping we'd stop in time. I was quite sure we would. It was a long field. The bungalow had a picture window. Our wheels were maybe ten feet off the ground and the window was growing larger. We touched down with a jolt, not half so bad as I'd expected. I slowed us, braking as hard as I dared, while the bungalow window came closer and closer, and a woman inside got up from her chair. She walked stiffly toward us, using a cane to improve her balance. Tall and slender, she wore a pale green sweater over brown pants and her white hair hung to her shoulders. She was separated from us by the glass of the window. A black hairband held her white hair back from her bony face. As we rolled toward her, she advanced toward us. She now stood so close to the glass that she could have stuck out her tongue and licked it if she'd wanted to. Our wheels stopped moving, right at the edge of her flowerbed. She was staring at our winged machine, and the next minute she was gone. I unstrapped myself, clambered out, and ran. The front door was unlocked. She'd landed on her side on the broadloom, missing the coffee table and its sharp corner. She'd not bled, and was breathing with her eyes closed, the pale green wool of her sweater moving up, then down, then up again the smallest bit as I knelt and spoke to her. I couldn't find any pulse in her wrist but I was maybe not pressing in the right spot. By then Bruce was crouching beside me, talking into his cellphone. Yes, an older woman, likely in her eighties, yes, breathing but non-responsive, no, we hadn't moved her. We sat on the floor, alongside her, waiting for the ambulance.

She had a name, of course. In her purse there were cards that named her, but I didn't go looking and neither did Bruce. We sat cross-legged on the floor. I kept expecting Bruce to say something revelatory, to make the perfect remark, not that I wanted him to, but in any case he failed to speak. He did not say, "Christ, what a fucking mess," or "Oh God, look what we've done, she mustn't die, she can't, please don't let her die, we didn't mean any harm." Nothing, not one word from Bruce's mouth. We knew where we were. We were at number 3477, Concession Road Nine, Dilson. Thanks to the GPS in Bruce's phone, we were not in a nameless house in a nameless field, and the ambulance would soon arrive, already it was racing along the highway, siren wailing. I glanced out the window at the ultralight, which was parked like a giant insect at the edge of her garden. Then I looked down at the soft sweater spread over her chest and her small belly. It was keeping her warm. But the sweater was no longer moving. I lowered my ear and I placed my hand on her chest. Not a whisper of air. I could detect no air entering or leaving her lungs. In the few seconds that my gaze had left her and wandered out the window, her heart had stopped beating and pumping. Tears were sliding down Bruce's pale cheeks. Mute, he stared at me. "Oh, God, oh, God," I kept repeating.'

'Oh, Maurice,' I murmured, and placed my hand on his. In all the years we'd been friends, I'd never touched his hand. Short hairs grew from his knuckles. His fingers had a fleshy density. His fingers were thicker than I expected and his skin very soft.

'Tell me a bit more. The ambulance arrived? The police were called?'

'Yes. Yes, of course.'

'And?'

'There will be a coroner's report.'

'You're not – ? I mean, they're not holding you responsible?'

'No. We called the ambulance the moment we found her, we touched nothing in her house, her purse was right there, all her money and cards intact, and the ultralight wouldn't start, had to be towed to the nearest airfield. No, no, in the eyes of the law I am innocent. That doesn't make me innocent. I've led a frivolous life, Julia.'

'Not entirely frivolous.'

'Thank you.'

'Maurice, you have to stop.'

'This is going to take me a while to figure out – my involvement. She lived alone. Her name is Elsa Burns. She was eighty-three. She has two daughters. One lives in Vancouver, the other in Toronto. I've spoken with the Toronto daughter.'

'You have?'

'I asked the police to tell any next of kin that I'd like to be in touch, and would they please offer my contact information. Fiona Burns called me. She visited her mother most weekends. She's proposed we meet. She wants to know more. I'm the last person, or rather Bruce and I are the last two people, to have seen her mother alive. She sounded surprisingly calm, Fiona Burns did, not exactly severe, but very precise. We're to meet tomorrow.'

'Nervous?'

'Absolutely. Will you go in my place? No, I don't mean that.'

'And Bruce?'

'He may or may not come. He's gone silent.'

'That doesn't sound good.'

'I'm giving him a few more days, then he's going to see a therapist.'

'Is he?'

'No discussion. I get that he doesn't want to talk to me. But he has to talk.'

'He won't talk to you, but he'll take your advice?'

'How should I know? I know nothing.'

'I'm sorry, Maurice.'

'This is not what I expected, the way he's reacting.'

'Can I help?'

'You are.'

Daisy

Oliver Bodinar, Clara Hodgkins, and I have signed a contract in triplicate. A copy for Oliver, one for Clara, and I in my role as Homsi get to keep one. Three signed documents declare that a novel titled *Don't Get Me Wrong* will be released ten months from now by Gimbal Books.

'The time frame is crazy. But anyone publishing books these days is certifiably insane, so why not get F. H. Homsi's masterpiece out there before one of us wakes up and tears the thing to pieces? It will win prizes, it will be translated into thirty languages, and Gimbal Books will get some long-overdue recognition for taking risks and delivering excellence. By some miracle, F. H. Homsi will be allowed to be F. H. Homsi, a reclusive writer who refuses to be interviewed or to attend award ceremonies. *Don't Get Me Wrong* is going to blow people's minds.'

Oliver wants to start editing tomorrow.

'She's not about to break the contract, is she? Not showing any signs? We do all the fine-tuning, copy-editing, design, promotion, then she decides to block the book from coming out?'

'No,' I assured him. 'She's arrived at each of our meetings on time. She trusts F. H. Homsi, and, most importantly, she wants Kamar to be known, to be appreciated, which can't happen unless the book comes out.'

Oliver shook a few pieces of candy-coated chewing gum into the palm of his hand, popped them in his mouth, and moved his jaw up and down with such deliberate slowness that I glanced at my watch to see at what speed the hands were moving, but Oliver's jaw had not taken control of time, not according to my watch. We were driving, or rather he was, while I watched him chew. We went over another speed bump and I tried to identify which parts of the car were rattling the loudest. Back left door and something underneath us.

'Do you ever chew gum when you're not driving?'

'No,' he claimed. 'Never.'

I adjusted the position of my leg. I wriggled my toes to verify that they would still wriggle upon request. Will Clara wriggle out of sight or worse, right when the book comes out? My toes offered me no answer. I did not want to dwell on the many possible ways that Clara might undermine her book, or that Oliver and I might do so for her. I did not want to think about the rage that would be aimed at me, when F. H. Homsi and I were discovered, as we were sure to be. I pictured my small, hard-won career going up in flames and the silence that would follow, the air full of ash. Soon I would be F. H. Homsi, whose work would outlive their outrage. To distract myself, I glanced out the window. Fine grains of snow were riding currents of air. The moment each grain touched the ground, it melted.

A hot bath relaxes the muscles. 'Your progress is excellent,' the physiotherapist tells me. I, however, am not convinced.

I know how far there is to go, months and months of exercises, and still I won't be able to walk half as well or as far as before. Fact. This is a fact. I'm not complaining. I am mourning. I am looking directly at the outcome. Every day my foot descends the wall with the same reluctance. This morning, I listened hard as my food slid down. But nothing came from next door, no sounds from Maurice or Bruce, nothing more about the woman whose death they believe they caused. I listened harder. The wall remained silent. I moved to the middle of the room. I am learning to march in place while balancing on a cushion. First you lift one leg, then the other, without toppling. I can now climb stairs, clutching the banister and alternating which leg leads: left, right, left, right. But when descending, only the right dares support me while the left foot drops through emptiness to the next stair below. Left, left, left is all I can do, coming down. Odd clicks. As the clicks are not painful, I attempt to ignore them. The calf feels wooden. The shape of a knee, my very own, has surfaced through the swelling. Also making itself known: the end of a metal bolt, a knob under skin, which my surgeon tells me I am to welcome into the family.

Maurice

I arrived early, found a table, and ordered a mint tea. A red wool coat, Fiona Burns had told me, I was to look for a short blond woman wearing a red wool coat. Still, as I surveyed the room, I hoped to locate a tall woman dressed in a pale green sweater, leaning on a cane, her white hair held back by a hairband, her eyes blue and staring at me – Elsa Burns alive and well.

The moment Fiona Burns appeared, short, blond, and wearing the coat she'd described, I stood up. She unbuttoned her coat and smiled at me.

'Thank you for agreeing to meet.'

'I am so, I can't say how…'

She sat and then I sat. She studied my face.

'I'm not here to make you feel guilty. What I would appreciate knowing is what you remember of my mother during the last minutes of her life.'

'She … she walked up to the window.'

'When?'

'As we were approaching in the ultralight. It's not exactly a plane, but two seats suspended from wings, with an engine, a steering wheel, and other controls. Your mother got up from her chair and walked toward us. The cloud coverage, the flat light, the angle of the sun – in any case, I could see in and she could see out. We were headed straight for her picture window. She stood on the other side of the glass. Our wheels had touched ground and we were slowing. I knew we wouldn't crash but I don't think she knew. Her expression was… On her face there was fear but also delight. Delight makes no sense, but I'm sure I saw it in her eyes, and in the corners of her mouth. A look of delight and disbelief, as if we weren't real, as if by pressing herself up to the glass she might discover if we actually existed or not. I could feel her examining my face. I wanted to gesture, to smile reassuringly. I wanted to tell her that our wheels would at most damage the outer edge of her garden, that she was safe. But I couldn't smile. I was too frightened. I hardly dared believe that we'd made it down out of the air. Like your mother, I wasn't yet sure we existed. Then she vanished. She fell out of sight. Her white, white hair, and her blue, blue eyes, and her pale green sweater, and her brown pants, and her cane – they were gone. As soon as I could unstrap myself I was out of the ultralight and running, and Bruce the same. We found her lying on her side on the broadloom. Luckily the front door was unlocked. The countryside, I thought, a place you needn't lock your door, not during the day, not when you're home. Her eyes were closed but she was breathing. She hadn't hurt her head. She'd missed the corner of the coffee table and had no visible wounds. But her bones, we couldn't tell about them, so we didn't move her. She was breathing. We sat on the floor beside her, Bruce with his phone to his ear and the 911 responder on the other end, asking, every few minutes, if we saw any changes. The ambulance was on its way. Then she stopped breathing. A few minutes later the paramedics were there.'

'Thank you. Your statement, the one you gave to the police, was quite complete, but hearing it from you is different. I know now that she wasn't alone. The moment I came in here and saw you, it all made sense. You have his eyes, his mouth, even the cleft in your chin belongs to him, and the shape of your nose. It's very unsettling. It wasn't you she saw through the window, sweeping down in your plane.'

Julia

No response to my emails – I don't see this as cause for panic. So many explanations are possible. Days go by without her leaving her apartment. A trip to the library to check for emails takes an effort of will, and the physical energy required to walk there and back, but mostly the strain of pushing her fears aside. 'We are very lucky,' I tell Alice, 'lucky that Clara takes her medications, that she can live more or less successfully on her own, eating who knows what, and washing her clothes, or not, figuring out a form of waterless hygiene of her own invention.'

Does she plug in the vacuum she asked me to buy for her, and make use of it? I warn her that her landlord might not be pleased, were he to drop by and discover how much dust she lets accumulate. What I consider a warning she calls a threat. 'It could be so much worse,' I tell Alice. 'Clara's frugal, and unlikely to be taken advantage of by some stranger posing as a friend. She trusts nobody. Still, she did visit you, and since her trip to St. Rita's and her happy encounter with Caesar the parrot, she's not sent me any messages asking us to back off. No such message. Which means she may visit you again.'

We are lucky. 'Clara's very determined and brave,' I tell Alice. But all of this Alice knows already.

Because she wasn't answering my emails, I dropped by Clara's apartment. Knock, knock. In the dimming glow and tranquility of the early evening, I perched on the top step of her front porch and fished for a pen and paper in my purse. 'Clara,' I wrote, 'Dropped by to see how you're doing. All well with Alice. You okay? Julia.'

Behind me, her door opened.

'Hi.'

She stepped out onto the porch, arms wrapped around her chest, chilly or scared or both.

'I was just going to tape this to your door.'

I handed her my note. She read it. Standing there in front of me, just like that, she read it.

'How am I? Not very well, in fact. I was hoping to see my psychiatrist, to ask for an extra session. Instead, she's taking time off. So I won't have even my regular session, and I've done something I wish I hadn't done.'

'Is there someone else you could see? Does your psychiatrist have someone to cover for her? How long will she be away? I'm asking you too many questions. Sorry.'

'She did give me a number, but I don't want to call a stranger. So long as I'm allowed to keep hiding, hiding helps.'

'I won't knock again. If you need to, call me?'

'Okay. Thanks.'

'Whatever it is you're regretting having done, would it help to tell me?'

'No. I don't think so. Thanks.'

'Good luck. Don't be too hard on yourself. I'll check in again.'

'I'll be fine, so long as I stay away from people.'

'Bye, Clara.'

'Bye, Julia.'

She turned and went back inside, closing and locking the door behind her. I stood in the still and luminous quiet on her top step, then descended to the sidewalk and went on my way.

Maurice

Yesterday, after two solid weeks of silence, of napping and non-action, Bruce pulled the Quran from his briefcase and remarked: 'I've never read this. My parents insisted, I refused. I'll read it now. I think I will. '

'Good idea.'

'And after the Quran, I'll read the Bible, then the Torah, also the Bhagavad Gita, and by then, who knows?' He took his reading glasses from his breast pocket and began to read.

I stood there grinning, dazed as a sunflower.

'You're speaking, Bruce! You can talk.'

'Yes. And now I've got reading to do. See you at lunch?'

'You wouldn't like to come for a walk?'

'Maurice.'

'Yes?'

'Leave me alone. I'm reading.'

'Bruce?'

'Yes?'

'She showed me a picture. Fiona Burns did. It looked just like me. It was of her father as a young man.'

'Have you got it? Show it to me.'

'She didn't give me the picture. She put it back in her wallet. He died when she was four years old. He was a bush pilot. Crashed somewhere in northern Ontario.'

Bruce removed his glasses, stared into space for a long moment, then put his glasses back on.

'Its more than I can take in right now, Maurice, you not being you but a dead bush pilot. I have reading to do. I don't plan to stop, not before lunch.'

Julia

'Stand up, stand up for Jesus.'

'What?'

'It came to me from somewhere. I must have heard it when I was little, maybe in school?'

Alice laughed, then sang again, the words from her childhood: 'Stand up, stand up for Jesus.'

I wheeled Alice through a set of doors and along the corridor leading to the exit.

'If you get chilly or bored, tell me, and we'll head back.'

In the narrow park, pigeons were perched on a low branch. They observed us as we went back and forth along the paved path.

'Pigeons on the grass, alas.'

'Where's that from?'

'Gertrude Stein.'

'Really? Any other poetry that you remember?'

'I walked fourteen miles. That's not poetry. But I did it. We were wearing saddle shoes and woollen skirts. I was with a friend. Who she was will come to me. The skirt rubbed and rubbed just below my knee, it made my leg sore and red, we walked for such a long time. '

'Are you chilly?'

'Yes, a bit.'

'Shall we go back inside?'

'I suppose the pigeons will be here next time. Or if they aren't, it doesn't matter. Yes, let's go in where it's warm. Pigeons in the park, alas, alas. I'd miss them if they weren't here next time but could forgive them.'

I wheeled Alice in and we waited for the elevator to arrive. Next to us a woman waited, hunched over her walker, her caregiver beside her. The hunched woman turned her head toward us, then explained her circumstances.

'My life is gone and I don't know what I've done with it. I'm quite well. I always am, that's the thing with me, I'm well, but I don't know where I am or what will happen next. I really have no idea. Whatever I did with my life, I hope I made good use of it. It's gone now. I must have done something with it.'

'Dora, you're on your way to your room. You've had dinner and now it's time to rest.'

The elevator doors opened and we all stepped in.

'Which floor?' asked the caregiver.

'Twelve, please,' said Alice. 'Pigeons on the grass alas. Pigeons on the grass alas. Short longer grass short longer longer shorter yellow grass. If they were not pigeons what were they. If they were not pigeons on the grass alas what were they.'

'You remember all that?'

'Stein. Gertrude Stein wrote all those words.'

'Do you like Stein?'

'We never met. If you mean her writing, not particularly.'

We arrived at the twelfth floor and I wheeled her along the corridor to her room.

'I never know what will surface. That's what keeps the days interesting, that and watching the people who come to look after me. I'd like someone to get me a map. Not you, Julia, you're busy. But someone.'

'How big a map would you like?'

'I don't know.'

'Of the world?'

'I'd like it to include the Philippines and Tibet.'

'I'll get you one.'

'Will you? Thank you.'

'A map is a good thing to have.'

'And Clara? Any news?'

'I spoke with her. She didn't want to talk for long. Her psychiatrist is away.'

'But you feel she's safe?'

'I do.'

Daisy

I was in my kitchen, concentrating on the elements of walking, when I heard my doorbell ring.

To achieve an even gait, swing your leg freely without involving your hip, do not forget to bend your leg at the knee, shift to your other leg but not too soon. Hum a funeral dirge under your breath to establish a rhythm.

I walked as evenly as I could across the kitchen, down the short hall, arrived at the door, and opened it. Clara Hodgkins stood on my porch, trembling.

'I'm sorry to disturb you, but I don't feel safe. May I come in?'

'Of course.'

We stood in the hall. I offered her tea, and to take her coat, which hung black and full. It descended to her ankles, and her wide-brimmed hat was made from felt of the same colour. She made no move to leave the hallway.

'It's just, my psychiatrist is away. Thanks for the offer of tea. I won't have any, but thank you. My psychiatrist is taking a few weeks off to cope with a death in her family. Not seeing her has made me more anxious than usual. I realize, now that it is too late, how foolish it was of me to approach you with my novel.'

'Foolish how? Are you sure you won't sit down?'

'I convinced myself that F. H. Homsi might allow me to participate. My psychiatrist, she's always pushing me to socialize. I've told her that my writing is the only way, the only possible route. She urged me to stop my private poetry, my language experiments she doesn't understand. I got tired of arguing with her. I've done my best to make myself comprehensible, and you have the results. I'm sorry. I don't trust you. I said I did, and thought I could. But my psychiatrist is away, and the inside of my head is not a good place.'

'When does your psychiatrist come back?'

'At the end of the month.'

'Would you consider waiting to make your final decision? You could decide after she gets back?'

'I'll try.'

'Are you sure you won't take your coat off? Come sit on the sofa.'

She perched on the edge, coat on.

'I've been rereading sections of your manuscript. Last night, the tale about the crow, the girl, and the judge, it got me thinking about my own childhood. I grew up with crows.'

'How so?' Clara asked, cocking her head and scrutinizing me.

'My father was a very shy man. The conversation of crows, their intelligence, fascinated him. He'd take me to the park, and the crows recognized him. He could imitate some of their calls and talked to them in a limited way.'

Immediately, she got up from the sofa and walked to the middle of the room, where she stood, hands twisting the brim of her hat.

'Crows,' I continued, 'they've often saved people's lives. My father was on holiday in British Columbia, driving on a mountain road, when a crow flew at the windshield, not just once but several times. The crow gave my father no choice but to pull onto the narrow shoulder. Around the next bend was a rock slide. Without the crow's warning, my father would have sailed around the sharp curve and crashed. Instead he got out of the car and investigated on foot while the crow flew above him, watching.'

'I don't want to be told anything more about crows.'

'I won't say any more.'

'Are you and Oliver Bodinar going to remove the tale of the crow, the girl, and the judge?'

'No, of course not.'

'I'm glad. I've got to go. I can let myself out. Don't get up. Thanks.'

'What shall I tell Oliver?'

'That I am unwell.'

'He knows. He wants to publish your manuscript, regardless.'

'He has poor judgment.'

'Once your psychiatrist is back, if you still want to withdraw your manuscript, please tell us as soon as possible. Does that sound fair, Clara?'

'Yes. Yes, it sounds fair.'

'Is there anything I can do to help? Please come over if you're feeling unsafe.'

'Crows are the only bird that can single you out, spot your face in a crowd, and tell their friends if you're dangerous or not. Did you know that? They're like primates wearing feathers, and I wish I could trust them, and talk to them the way your father does.'

'Could you trust a crow better than a person?'

'Possibly. I'd have to think about that. The U.S. Department of Defense is funding research on crows. They must be planning to use them in some horrible way. Crows are like us. They're smart and self-serving. I'll give you my answer about my manuscript as soon as I can. Thank you for your patience. Goodbye, Daisy.'

Julia

I banged on Clara's door. I'd told her I wouldn't, that I'd let her hide. But the more I thought about her psychiatrist being away, and Clara having done something she regretted doing, the more anxious I became. I waited. No answer. No curtain twitch. I gave up, went home.

Maurice

Fiona Burns has requested a second meeting with me. This alarming news arrived by email. I have consented.

Dear Maurice,

If you can spare the time, I'd like to speak with you again. Might you be available tomorrow at two in the afternoon? We could meet in the same café as last time? I apologize for the short notice and look forward to receiving your answer.

Regards, Fiona Burns.

You'd hardly think I'd caused her mother's death. Her tone both calms and unnerves me. Fiona Burns and I are to meet for lunch tomorrow. I will again sit and face the daughter of my victim.

Daisy

The leg's progress felt uncertain. The leg's progress looked uncertain. Today, the leg succumbed, and the foot slid further below the pencil mark than ever before.

As I witnessed the foot repeating its new accomplishment, Bruce's voice slipped, melodious, through the wall. He was reading aloud from a text by Simone Weil: 'There is true desire when there is an effort of attention. It is truly light that is desired if all other motives are absent. Even if the efforts of attention remained apparently sterile for years, one day a light exactly proportional to these efforts shall inundate the soul.'

Clara

This morning, a computer became free and I claimed it, I plugged in my earbuds. The moment I did so, the librarian stood up behind her desk. She did not look directly at me, but this was perhaps a ploy. Her oddly flat face was beautiful. It was smooth and round, a soothing shape for a face, or for anything. I lowered my head as she approached the bank of public terminals. I'd used my own earbuds before and not been reprimanded for breaking any rule, but she was new or was new to me. I wanted to look up and gaze at her flat face, the round shape of it. Instead I stared at the floor. She was now separated from me by inches of air. Into the little box, placed between two of the terminals, she dropped a handful of short pencils. Then she walked away without commenting on my earbuds. She did not step away from me quickly. The oddity of my clothes, therefore, had not signalled danger, had not suggested infection, the spread of my invisible disease. I raised my head. She was seated once more behind the information desk, her head bowed. The internoose behaved as it always does, opening then tightening, pulling me into its maze. I stabbed at the too-many samples of crows cawing. I opened pages, slid them over each other, listened to layers of beating wings, of crows in woods, of cawing on city bridges, of crows in parking lots, and of crows in corn fields, until their cawing swallowed the library. The deeper I fell, the brighter their cries became. Then all of it ended. I opened my eyes. I clicked on new links: 'Pre-feeding Caw,' 'Rattle or Comb Caw,' 'Alarm call.' A careful classification of auditory specimens exists.

Though no sample lasted more than a few seconds, each succeeded. Each removed me from the library. I was dropped inside a cry that pried open the sky. Another, with higher notes, operated with surgical precision. I did not feel attacked but addressed by an orator I longed to understand. By the time my hour was up, the crows had made bell sounds, drips, clicks, rattles. I didn't know the names of the other sounds. My time was up. No more shining rawness. No more tumbling. I removed my earbuds and stood there, expelled from the world of crows. I stood there, telling myself: *Next time, look at who's talking to you. Beak and eye and claw attached to language. You should never have listened to Daisy. Beak and eye and claw. You've got to figure them out before they figure you out. If you knew what they were saying.* My head was crowded with crow. I reserved another computer session, but it wouldn't start for another half-hour. I went off into the stacks. 'Don't forget,' Kamar whispered, 'they're thieves. Remember the molasses. Remember what they did to you.' I found and opened *Rutherford's Guide to Birds of North America.* A sleek head stared at me, its eye shiny and knowing. I kept the book open. I examined the alignment of the feathers, the polished beak, the tilt of its neck, and warned Kamar to keep her thoughts to herself, but she only whispered louder. I figured her out, I figured her in. I out-figured her. She was punishing me, because now I wasn't going to give her to Daisy and Oliver, and she wanted to get away from me. I pulled out a pen. *Shut the fuck up*, I wrote in large letters across page 89 of

Rutherford's Guide to Birds of North America to prevent myself from shouting at Kamar, because shouting in the library is not a good thing, but she went right on moaning her blind pain, tightening her fear around my throat, so I dug the pen into the bird's eye, and I closed the book and hurried down the stairs, and down the stairs, and past the long tables supporting the rows of computers where I'd booked my second hour and the crows were waiting for me, and out through the security gate, bag thrown open, nothing to hide, screaming at the guard but with my mouth clamped shut so he couldn't hear and stop me from returning tomorrow. Out I burst onto the sidewalk, where I was free to hiss at the pavement: 'I am not a fucking thief. Stop staring at me. She means the crows. Don't look at me. You don't know shit about me.'

Daisy

This table I now think of as 'ours,' the one nearest the window. Clafouti and Clara have become inseparable for me. Despite her anxiety, the real author of *Don't Get Me Wrong* has decided to publish her manuscript, as planned. She is not waiting for her psychiatrist's return. She wants to move forward, provided the subject of crows is disallowed from any future conversation. She and F. H. Homsi have agreed to a fixed pattern of encounters. The more regular and reliable an arrangement, the more reassuring, she's explained. They will meet every second Tuesday here, at Clafouti. F. H. Homsi will report that the editing is progressing well, or not progressing, and offer whatever other news. Soon Oliver will show Homsi a few possible designs for the cover, which Homsi will describe to Clara.

This afternoon, she brought me flowers – daisies. The barista offered to stand them in water. *A lot, a little, not at all, a lot, a little*. Yank off the oracular white petals. I did so often as a teenager. Back then I wanted *a lot* or *not at all*. *A little* struck me as pointless. The daisies, standing in a mason jar on our table, have such long stems and nodding heads.

'You are important to me,' announced Clara. She looked me in the eyes as she said this, then she threw her gaze away from me so as not to witness my reaction. I waited. Again her eyes confronted mine. 'I never want to meet Oliver Bodinar. Homsi's job is to keep him away from me, to keep everyone away from me.'

'Understood. Homsi understands.'

'Thank you. Please thank Homsi.'

'I will.'

'Have Homsi and Oliver begun editing?'

'Yes.'

'And Homsi is happy?'

'Homsi and Bodinar work well together. Homsi and Bodinar are exacting editors but respectful, and they find there's little to change. They are enjoying the precision of your prose, also the loose moments when the words seem released from under great pressure and syntax explodes. Kamar's thoughts land in patterns that make no immediate sense, but Homsi and Bodinar are succumbing to the book's logic.'

'Good. I am glad. I am glad for Kamar's sake. But I need to stop talking about this. Kamar is making me anxious. She turned on me a few days ago.'

'Kamar? What did she do?'

'Never mind. Forget it.'

'Your psychiatrist. She'll be back soon?'

'Two weeks from now.'

'Having her back will be reassuring?'

'Yes. But we don't always get along.'

'Did you say there was a death in the family?'

'Her mother.'

'That will have been hard on her, I imagine.'

'It will be confusing. She's good. She's as good a psychiatrist as I've ever found, but still I have to keep things clear. I don't know how well she knows herself. I've been wondering how she's experiencing her mother's death. She may be seeing in her mother's death a glimpse of her own mortality – that would make sense. She could also be floating, freed of decades of guilt, of inability to plug the hole in her mother. She's never spoken to me about her mother. But there have been clues. The hole she refused to stop up with love. I don't make the mistake of assuming I know her better than I do. She makes assumptions about me all the time. She crosses certain lines. She may get away with that sort of behaviour with other patients, but not with me. I catch her out. I'm not saying I'm any smarter. We're pretty well-matched. She's an agile ambusher. It's a complicated game, and we're playing for keeps. Sometimes she enrages me to the point I figure I'll never see her again. But I couldn't survive without her. Or maybe she's just learned to make me feel that way.'

Clara glanced down at her wristwatch.

'It's later than I thought. I've got to go. My coffee's paid for.'

She buttoned her jacket, pushed back her chair, and left.

An afterimage of her grey eyes filling with panic floated in the café. I manoeuvred my leg out from under the table and paid my bill. Carrying a bouquet of daisies, I walked slowly home.

Clara

Does friendship exist between Daisy and me? I think she likes Us. But this can't be, since she sees only Me, not Us. She can't know about Us, can't and mustn't. What if Daisy is one of Them? Until this afternoon, she likely liked my likeness. But it fell from its frame. Julia and Daisy must never meet. My sister would not tolerate Daisy's interest in Me, she could not allow Me a friendship outside her control. If Daisy were to learn about Us and to tell Julia about Us, Julia would send the Emotionals to drown Us in a Sea of Histrionics. They have plans for Our body. Which of Us does Daisy see and hear? I try to speak as Clara, as Me, to always be Clara when We are with Daisy. The trouble is Our amnesia. WE MUST NOT REMEMBER: of sealing wax and kings. 'What do you think you're doing?' asked Julia, and we had to stop, because Julia is one of them and they are too numerous. We could not stick our fingers up all their noses at once. They carry their buckets of shit with them. Beatrix brought butter tarts. We'd rowed out into the middle of the lake, when she stood and bared her bum. We didn't mind drowning. The practice of drowning is approved of and often put to use for retrieving information that has been swallowed whole and is wholly indigestible, though believed by some to be holy. A fine must be paid if death occurs before the missing pieces are recovered. The size of the fine depends on the fireman's mood. A recent manual, government-approved, recommends tying a cat to the top of the informant's head. As the water rises, the cat will claw the unfortunate's ears. Clawing of the ears stimulates speech, if the day is not overly humid. Birdsong encourages collusion. To discourage partisans from hiding in the foliage of public parks, all birds are to be shot if seen wearing feathers. Julia has been sent to spy on me. I used to think she was one of Us, but she is one of Them. Blow the bag up. Not the woman, the paper bag. I only meant the paper bag.

Julia

The grave has been dug – a hole in the dirt, artificial grass unrolled along its lip. A mound of loose soil waits off to one side. Long and deep the hole is, its dense walls alive with roots and insects. Into this space she will be lowered. Elsa Burns. I did not know her. I am here to support Maurice, who is having a hard time freeing himself of the idea that he killed her, Maurice who has not yet arrived. I've come early because I'm anxious. This is the correct grave, I hope. To calm myself, I think I'll climb that path over there, the one leading to the summit of the grassy knoll, and sit under that oak tree at the very top.

Still no sign of Maurice, for whose sake I am waiting for this funeral, which refuses to get underway. Seen from up here, from this summit, the hole in the ground looks much smaller but just as raw, as new and intrusive as when I was standing down there. The hole invites. It begs completion. Aha, here comes the hearse and a cortege of several cars. Still no Maurice. From a dark limousine two women are extricating themselves. Elsa Burns's daughters? The short blond one is wearing a red coat. She must be Fiona. Maurice has mentioned repeatedly a red coat. Here comes another car, small and white. It's advancing slowly, with as much dignity as such a tiny vehicle is capable of. It's come to a halt. Ah, Maurice! He's emerging from the passenger side, and from behind the wheel long-legged Bruce is sliding out with inexplicable ease. On his feet are his two-tone shoes, of course, recently polished, by the gleaming look of them. Bruce and Maurice, at last. They are glancing about, getting their bearings. Now they're walking over to the woman in the red coat. It's time for me to join them. A taxi has pulled up. I'll stroll discreetly down the hillside. Wait! Clara? Oh, my God, it's Clara. I can't go down there. Clara, attending a funeral? Already the taxi is driving off. There's a woman with a cane. She and Clara are stepping off the road and into the grass. Who is that woman with my sister? They are hanging back, Clara and her friend with the cane. Clara has a friend? Why has she brought Clara here? Oh, God, I am dense. Fiona Burns. Fiona of the red coat must be Clara's psychiatrist. How many times have I asked Alice for the name of Clara's psychiatrist? As if Alice could remember. But she might have. It could have surfaced at any moment. Where are Maurice and Bruce? Oh, there they are, way over there next to Dr. Fiona Burns and her sister and the other mourners. They've assembled at the edge of the grave. The moment has come for me to join Maurice, this is when I ought to be slipping my arm through his. I promised to be there. Soon the preacher will speak, and possibly Bruce also. I'll hear nothing from this stupid hilltop. But I can't go down. Clara, startled, taken off guard, might behave who knows how? Clara has made a friend! What a great flapping of wings! Three crows have just landed in the branches above me. Strikingly at ease they are, in their permanent funeral attire. One of them is returning my stare. What a chorus of cawing. What's going on below? If only I had a pair of binoculars. Clara is turning her head. Her gaze is gliding up the hill and now she's seen me. Oh, Christ, she's running off between the trees, away, away. The woman with the cane – how long can she balance there, left on her own, swaying uncertainly? Should I go to her, or run after Clara? Grab Maurice by the arm and ask his advice? I am running. Catch her, catch her, catch her if I can. Each breath slicing between my ribs, the grass flattening beneath my feet, down the slope I go, hurtling along the level now, until the next small rise, and she's keeping ahead of me. No. She's stopped. She's turned. She's staring at me and shouting. Her words are arriving meaningless. My fear has carved a trench, a delay that comprehension must leap across. Meaning has leapt and arrived: 'Stay back. Stay back. Don't come near me.' If I sit down on the grass right now, she'll understand, she'll know that I know that she does not want me to pursue her. But my legs refuse. She is yelling, eyes searching for an exit. She's off again, has slipped between two bushes, is going out through the cemetery gates and down Mount Pleasant Road, running, running, searching for an escape from me, an exit.

Maurice

You? Charging full tilt across the hillside? This is not, absolutely not, what we agreed upon. Elsa Burns in a box being lowered into the ground, and your arm slipped through mine – that was the plan, Julia my dear. What in God's name? First you fail to appear, then you spring into existence as motion blur in the corner of my eye. If you'd not been moving so fast, I'd have missed you. There I stood, feeling full of shame, and pissed off at you. It was your idea that you come. You offered your moral support. 'I'll be at the burial, I want to be there for you.' When Bruce and I arrived, no sign of you. Fiona and her sister we spotted immediately. Bruce stepped forward and announced that he'd like to read a small passage from the Bhagavad Gita, to which Fiona, more quiet than usual, nodded her head in consent. Then the minister approached and requested a word with both daughters. I turned my back to give them privacy and to survey the surrounding area, hoping to see you arrive on foot or step out of a car. Instead, who arrives? Clara, your sister! You must have seen her, from up on your hill, seen her climb out of the taxi, and with her Daisy Harding, Bruce's other-side-of-the-wall neighbour. I stood there, feeling the wind against my skin, thinking what a terrible day it would be for flying, and wondering if I'd ever want to go up in the ultralight again, and trying to figure out why on earth Daisy Harding was with your sister, and what were they both doing here, and why hadn't you told me that your sister was coming, or didn't you know, and where the hell were you, when the minister began his speech, and my thoughts changed track, and our little throng, from which those two stood apart, tightened around the grave, and we all bowed our heads in concentration. I could no longer see Fiona's downturned face, nor her sister's. I killed their mother. You insist that I didn't, but I did. Beside me stood Bruce, nervously fingering the paper in his pocket. I'd watched him copying from one holy book after another, before settling on the lines of Hindu wisdom now concealed in his pocket. Soon, soon, he'd pull out the paper, open his mouth, and say aloud his frightened farewell to Elsa of the pale green sweater and brown slacks, 'dead from shock and delight,' or so her daughter claims. 'My mother died in a state of wonder,' insists Dr. Burns, mender of minds, doctor made small by death, doctor weeping. A sudden, raucous cawing yanked our attention, and there you were, observing us from your hilltop. Immediately Clara broke free. She shot past us, feet pounding on the path.

The minister turned his head and watched her go. All heads were turning. Down the slope and straight for us you charged, Julia dear. But you were not descending to apologize or to explain. You swerved east, in pursuit of Clara, extending your stride, hair flying, and there I was, running also, calling out, shouting not your name but Clara's. 'Clara, stop. It's all right, Clara, it's all right.' I don't know why her name, not yours. She most certainly couldn't hear me. It was your name I should have been calling. 'Julia, stop. It's all right, Julia, it's all right.'

Daisy

The entire fiasco was stupid and avoidable. It was me who encouraged Clara, who offered to go with her. This broken leg has taught me nothing. The day was far too windy for anything to go as expected, clouds sweeping across the sky, trees bending. I leaned on my cane and thought about the wild audacity of humans, our determination to stand upright on two legs. My thoughts made me laugh. 'What's so funny?' asked Clara, suspicious as always. 'Standing. The absurdity of being vertical,' I answered. Clara grinned. Her happiness gave me pleasure. A gust of wind high above us shifted the clouds and the sky became bright and I looked all around me. I saw grass and trees, and Bruce and Maurice, my two neighbours. The wind had deposited them beside a birch tree, at the edge of the grave of Clara's psychiatrist's mother. Why had I not put two and two together earlier? 'I know that man with the fancy shoes,' I whispered to Clara, 'and the man beside him, they live on the other side of my living room wall. The one with the shoes is Bruce Mammadov, an Australian; the other is Maurice, whose last name I don't know. You may have seen them when you were coming or going from my front porch?' Clara shook her head. She continued shaking her head, and her hands began searching the air for an answer until she succeeded in pointing her finger at Maurice. 'My sister, he's her best friend.' Her entire being was now visibly trembling in fury and fear. 'I should never have fucking come here.' She dug her heel into the ground. 'Dr. Burns can't want me here. Why would she want to have one of her patients turn up at her mother's burial? What a stupid idea. I'm an idiot. I get Maurice as my prize for being so stupid. I have to leave. I'm sorry. I thought I could do this but I can't. This is my fault. I wanted to know how Dr. Burns would behave, confronted by her mother's grave. I wanted to see her fall apart. Now I get to pay for sticking my nose where it didn't belong. If Maurice walks over here, I'll have to leave, I'll have to abandon you, I'm sorry, but I won't have any choice.'

I advised Clara to wait and catch her breath. I suggested that her presence, possibly, might comfort Dr. Burns, might send a message of validation in a moment of loss. I proposed that our mutual decision to attend the burial of Elsa Burns was neither stupid nor inappropriate, while in my ears all I could hear was the whistling of wind, then Clara, staring at the ground, started a tuneless humming under her breath. She wrapped her arms around her middle, then lifted her head and looked me in the eye. 'You're right. I do care about Dr. Burns. A lot. I care about her a lot.' Tears were sliding down Clara's cheeks and along the edge of her nose. They went slipping into her mouth. She covered her face. I fished in my pocket for a Kleenex. Scraps of eulogy sailed over to us, clusters of words carried on the wind. Handfuls of soil were being dropped into a deep, rectangular hole, dirt raining down on the coffin of Elsa Burns. From high in a tree, several crows called out in solidarity. Clara turned her attention to the crows. On the crest of the hill stood a woman. As if shot from a gun, Clara took off. Within seconds the woman on the hill started running, racing down, racing Clara toward some finish line visible to no one but the two of them.

Maurice

We caught up with Julia. She was sitting on the ground, alone.

'Gone?' I asked, and Julia nodded. We placed ourselves, Bruce and I, on either side of her, like two hapless sentinels. The groaning of ancient trees urged patience. 'I'm an idiot,' she announced. Just then, Daisy Harding came lurching toward us, her gait uneven, her cane preventing her from toppling. She perched her weary self on a tombstone a few feet away.

'Julia Hodgkins, Daisy Harding. Daisy, Julia,' I offered. It was all I felt capable of.

'Where's Clara?' asked Daisy.

We could pursue Clara or not. She was out there, running through the city, demons far worse than us howling inside her. Soberly, we debated. We arrived at the following plan: Daisy would ride with Bruce in his car to the Leslie Street Spit, and there the two of them would search a tiny portion of the shore of Lake Ontario. The Leslie Street Spit was Daisy's idea. Farther north, a streetcar would carry Julia and me along St. Clair Avenue to the stop closest to Clara's apartment, where we'd get off. Should Clara fail to respond when we knocked on her door, Julia would use her emergency key to let us in, and from the front hall we'd call out Clara's name. Further failure to answer on Clara's part would justify our entering further, to verify if she was indeed not home or perhaps unconscious and in need of immediate assistance. By cellphone, the two search parties would communicate their findings to each other.

Bruce and I ran, we ran back the way we'd come, along the weaving path between wind-flailed trees, back to Elsa's grave, to get Bruce's car, I gasping for breath, determined to keep abreast of my long-legged darling.

Daisy

Here is where Kamar drowned herself. The Spit. A finger built from discarded concrete, shattered toilet bowls, old crockery, and broken sewage pipes. A rubble digit, overgrown in patches, colonized by willows and aspen, grasses, asters, and bulrushes. It pokes into the lake and the frigid water slaps at it.

My cane and unwilling leg slowed us down. At first we saw no sign of Clara.

Maurice

Words painted on the walls, crude caricatures of the heads of animals, of the heads of birds, alongside faceless children of various sizes. And there were dolls hanging by their feet, strips of paper uncurling from their abdomens. It surpassed what I'd expected in horror, sadness, and artistry. Julia had warned me, but nothing could have prepared me for the grief I felt. Words typed on these gut streamers, words I did not bend close enough to read. Inscribed in red strokes of paint above the unusable fireplace: *Say not what you see.* In a thicker black scrawl descending the living room wall: *Those who tell shall be blinded. Do not swallow. Beware the emotional deluge. I am the other eye.*

In flowing blue cursive on the wall outside the bathroom: *Of sealing wax and kings.* In her bedroom, on the inside of her closet door: *If Clara.* In the bathroom stood the unused bathtub, its once-long-ago-white surface licked by thick tongues of paint, and above the tub, from the ceiling hung a black fishnet stocking, stuffed full of dead light bulbs.

Clara everywhere but nowhere, we locked her door behind us.

Daisy

Mismatched houses line up in pairs. The brilliant green garbage truck grinds and compresses its cargo of refuse as it glides up the street. How is it that this truck's appearance and the sounds it produces, the turning of its rubber wheels, the gnashing of its metal teeth, and the rumble of its engine, combine to convince me of its reality? For Clara the houses outside my window are a hoax, a facade thrown together to trick her. The entire street, visual and audible, has been devised by an organization devoted to the torture of children and defective adults. A defective adult may be one who trusts too easily or one incapable of trust. She cannot say when she first became aware that such a plot exists. Her childhood she can rarely reach inside of, and when she does she retrieves little. Were her cocooned past to hatch, the monster of pain released would be of giant proportions, or so she fears. Into the jaws of her past she would disappear forever. This much she has explained to me.

I poured us each more tea. I rubbed my sore leg. She saw my hand moving back and forth and asked if I was in pain.

'No,' I assured her. 'An aching stiffness, that's all. It feels wooden, and the tips of the metal screws trouble me when I touch them through my skin. But it's recovering. It's functioning.'

I did not tell her: I know who put them there, those screws; I remember being wheeled into the operating room and staring up at an arrangement of lights that resembled the underbelly of a UFO or the eye of a giant fly, and I remember feeling grateful that many lights were to shine down on my flesh as the surgeon cut my leg open, and I recall that I had no doubts as to why he was about to insert metal plates inside my shattered limb, and I know that I gave my consent. Might another surgeon have performed the operation better? This doubt I do toy with. When my leg hurts, I imagine a more pleasing outcome, and I attribute varying degrees of incompetence to my surgeon. However, the hospital's excellent reputation suggests that I was not placed in poor hands, and most importantly, my leg's steady progress indicates that the surgery was well-executed. I banish my fears, or rather I juggle them. A cataloguing of my worries occurs most often when I'm lying in bed and confronted by night's borderless expanse or the demanding arrival of daylight. A rapid, desperate sorting of my terrors may occur on a public bus also, or while I'm seated on this sofa and pretending to read.

As I turned these thoughts over, trying to decide if knowing of my vulnerabilities would be of use or detrimental to Clara, I watched her drink her tea in great gulps and set down her cup. She lifted the pot to pour herself more, making a visible effort not to allow the tremor in her hand to cause any liquid to spill onto the table.

'Cruelty, justifiably provoked by my own despicability,' she said, 'it allows the world to remain a potentially desirable place to live, though not for me, as I am despicable.' Her fingers smoothed the cloth of her skirt where it spread over her knees. 'If, however, I am the innocent victim of monstrous misuse,' she continued, 'then I am not despicable, but the world becomes an even greater palace of horrors, of human viciousness set loose. I take either path, depending on the hour or the day, and either way I find myself impaled upon an event or a series of repeated events that I cannot remember. Last week, on the Leslie Street Spit, when you and your neighbour found me, I wasn't going to drown myself, not unless Julia had come looking for me. I wanted to be near water. I also needed to be as far from Julia as I could get. I wanted waves. It was windy enough. The sound of waves is a good place to hide.'

'Why are you afraid of Julia?' I asked.

'I'm afraid of everyone,' said Clara, fixing me with her weather-station eyes. 'But Julia has more reason to shut me up, to control and silence me, than you do. She witnessed what was done to me and does not want to remember. I used to feel sorry for her. I wanted to protect her. But now I understand that her desire to forget makes her dangerous. To remember would be like falling out a window, for her. She might not recover.'

Clara straightened her skirt and adjusted her scarf, then asked me, 'Knowing me as you do now, are you still willing to publish my book?'

Maurice

I returned her call immediately. I'm sure that she heard the nervousness in my voice.

'Dr. Burns? Dr. Burns?' I said her name twice.

'Hello, Maurice. I'd rather you call me Fiona, if you don't mind.'

'Hello, Fiona.'

'Thank you. I have a favour to ask of you.' Her tone became even quieter, more firm. 'Would you take me for a ride in your ultralight?'

The answer I gave included the words *pleasure* and *maximum stillness*. That much I know. I've accepted to take her up into the air on a windless afternoon. Bruce is against it. He's searching the Torah at this very moment, scouring the text for a quotation that might dissuade me from carrying out Dr. Burns's plan.

'I want you to fly me over the farm and land exactly as you did on the day my mother died. She saw you coming toward her. She mistook you for my father. As soon as you've brought us down, and our front wheels are touching the edge of her garden, I'll get out and go into the house. I'll wait in the living room, at the window, while you fly back up and repeat the landing. That's my wish. It's a lot to ask, I realize.'

Once Dr. Burns is strapped into her seat and wearing her helmet, up we'll go. Tomorrow at three in the afternoon, weather permitting, we'll roll across the stubble, then rise into the air.

Julia

The others appeared to be working, heads bent in concentration. I felt my eyes close then open. On the screen hung my incomplete response to an email enquiry from a hopeful artist. I'd slept poorly the night before and now it was late afternoon. I was accomplishing nothing. I opened my desk drawer and lifted out the book of votive paintings given to me by Clara. A man was tumbling through the creamy air, a sixth-storey window open above him. He was clutching a wooden shutter and wore a look of disbelief on his face. On the following page, two children were plummeting headfirst, side by side, having fallen from the spiral staircase of an Italian villa. Though I examined them closely, the children were too small for me to make out the expressions on their faces.

Notes and Acknowledgments

A series of fictional votive paintings by artists Adam Broomberg and Oliver Chanarin inspired this novel, as did Alexander Pilis's installation *Architecture Prallax: Through the Looking Glass* (Koffler Gallery, 2015), followed by a fall from a bicycle, and the viewing online of true votive paintings from Genoa. The two Syrian folk tales retold by F. H. Homsi in *If Clara* were collected in the streets of Aleppo by Samir Tahhan, translated into English by Andrea Rugh, and can be found in *Folktales from Syria*, published by the Centre for Middle Eastern Studies, The University of Texas at Austin, 2004. I thank Peggy Gough of the University of Texas Press and Dena Afrasiabi of the Centre for Middle Eastern Studies, the University of Texas at Austin, for their generous assistance.

I thank Greg Sharp, Eva H. D., Emma Moss Brender, Sarah Mangle, Mariella Bertelli, Anne Egger, Kate Cayley, Joanne Schwartz, and Guy Ewing for reading this novel at various stages, for expressing faith in it, and for seeing what I could not see.

Thank you to my most understanding agent, Samantha Haywood, who has stuck with me these many years. Thank you to my wise and wonderful editor, Alana Wilcox, who can hear a mouse scurrying under snow and whose head, I suspect, can revolve 360 degrees. Thanks to everyone at Coach House. Thank you to David Gressot, my editor at Actes Sud, for his insights. Boundless thanks to my family: Mary Jane, Jonno, Emma, and Christina.

Martha Baillie's previous novel, *The Search for Heinrich Schlögel*, was an *O* magazine Editors' pick, and was published in France by Actes Sud. Her 2009 novel, *The Incident Report*, was nominated for the Scotiabank Giller Prize. Her poetry has been featured in the *Iowa Review* and her non-fiction in *Brick* magazine and Longreads. She has written about contemporary visual art for the Art Gallery of Ontario and the Koffler Gallery. Her multimedia project, *The Schlogel Archive*, shown at the Koffler Gallery in 2015, was selected by *NOW* magazine as a Contact Festival 'Must See,' and can be visited at www.schlogel.ca. Martha was born in Toronto, has lived in Scotland and France, has hiked in the Arctic, and has travelled extensively in Asia. She now lives and works in Toronto.

Typeset in Whitman

Printed at the Coach House on bpNichol Lane in Toronto, Ontario, on Zephyr Antique Laid paper, which was manufactured, acid-free, in Saint-Jérôme, Quebec, from second-growth forests. This book was printed with vegetable-based ink on a 1973 Heidelberg KORD offset litho press. Its pages were folded on a Baumfolder, gathered by hand, bound on a Sulby Auto-Minabinda and trimmed on a Polar single-knife cutter.

Edited and designed by Alana Wilcox
Cover design by Ingrid Paulson

Coach House Books
80 bpNichol Lane
Toronto ON M5S 3J4
Canada

mail@chbooks.com
www.chbooks.com

800 367 6360
426 979 2217